He looked up again to see the cursor slowly travelling upwards – level 1... 2... 3... Pete stared, suddenly scared. He had no control over this game. *"Get out of here!"* his brain screamed at him, and he started to wrestle with the headset again. But the clasp still wouldn't budge. He tried to step off the grey mat beneath his feet, but some invisible force yanked him back. And all the time the cursor was climbing upwards 4... 5... 6... until it stopped at number 7.

Level 7. This was the place where Rick's memories were stored. But what was he supposed to do now? He couldn't play the game – the joystick was bust. He couldn't stop the machine – the helmet was locked. He was trapped – trapped inside the *Mindmaster*...

Other titles in this series

MINDMASTER

Clive Gifford

From an original idea by Tony Allan

First published in 1996 by Usborne Publishing Ltd, Usborne House, 83-85 Saffron Hill, London EC1N 8RT, England.

Copyright © 1996 Usborne Publishing Ltd.

The name Usborne and the device are Trade Marks of Usborne Publishing Ltd.

ISBN 0 7460 2470 3 (paperback)

ISBN 0 7460 2471 1(hardback)

Typeset in Palatino

Printed in Great Britain

Series Editor: Gaby Waters

Editor: Michelle Bates

Designer: Lucy Parris

Cover illustration: Barry Jones

CONTENTS

1

Memories

One-nil! Three minutes left. The captain trapped the ball on the halfway line. Sprinting forward, he dodged one tackle, then another. He looked up. Both his strikers were marked. Only one thing to do. Swerving, he raced into the penalty area. The goalie was advancing. In a split second, he unleashed a rocket of a shot. For a moment it looked wide. But no, it slammed into the net. The crowd cheered. Two-nil!

Pete Clark rubbed his brown eyes and ran his fingers through his hair. He watched as his friend, Jez Harris, let go of the game controller, leaned back and drank in the computer-generated applause.

"You see Pete, I'm a football hero too," said Jez.

Pete grinned. It was true. In his own room, on his

32 bit games machine, Jez was indeed a football star.

"It's nothing like the real thing," protested Pete.

"No," muttered Jez. "It's better."

The game restarted and Jez went quiet.

Pete looked around Jez's room. Calling it a mess was being kind. It looked like a bomb had hit a computer store. Games magazines, disks and cartridges were strewn everywhere.

Jez's soccer game ended. He punched the air in victory. "Your turn," he said, handing Pete his worn Pro Gamepad.

"Not now," Pete replied, looking at his watch. It was six-thirty. He'd promised Mum he'd be home half an hour ago.

"Come on. Quick game of *Splat Attack*?" Jez urged, rummaging around the mess for a different disk.

"Nah. I'm late already, Jez," said Pete.

Jez put on his disappointed face, the one he'd perfected ever since he'd started getting spotty, just after his stepmother moved in. But Pete wouldn't be swayed.

"Next time," he said, walking to the front door. Jez nodded and sighed.

Pete sprinted all the way from Jez's house back home to Ferndown Road. He sometimes wondered what made him and Jez best friends – they were so completely different. Where he was into football, Jez was a real computer freak.

Pete had never really been into computer games.

He'd played a few on Jez's console and he'd often hung around with him at the arcades on the High Street, but somehow they never seemed that exciting, well... not compared with football.

"You're late, Peter," Mum muttered as he stepped through the front door, but she was too busy to start lecturing him. She had to get to work. "I've got a late shift tonight. I told you this morning... remember? Can you..."

"Look after your younger brother?" Pete interrupted, finishing off her sentence. "And make sure he does his reading and goes to bed early."

"Well, you want new football boots don't you?" she said, pulling on her jacket.

Pete nodded and sighed.

As the front door slammed, Pete's younger brother, Tommy, came bolting down the stairs. "Can we play football, Pete, can we?" His bright blue eyes peered out from under his blond fringe.

"Go on then," said Pete. "Out in the back garden but don't tell Mum."

Tommy grinned manically and sprinted through the house.

Poor Tommy, thought Pete. He was all right for a kid brother, but he was finding schoolwork impossible. He couldn't even recognize his letters. Pete fiddled with some of Tommy's word cards, lying on the kitchen table.

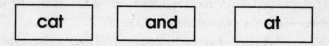

He'd been learning these words for weeks now.

Pete walked out onto the back lawn and stared ahead. The houses in Ferndown Road were small but they had large back gardens. Pete's gaze drifted over to the greenhouse in the far corner of the garden. He glanced fondly at the dilapidated old building. Half a dozen panes of glass were missing, the door was off its hinges and most of the wooden frame was rotting away but it still stood there.

His dad had been in charge of the garden – not that he'd done a lot apart from mowing the lawn. The greenhouse had been his special, private place – where he'd escaped to get some peace and quiet. Pete let a collection of pleasant memories of his dad waft through his mind. He often did this now, but he tried not to go over the accident or dwell on Dad not being there, despite the constant reminders – almost no pocket money, his mum being at work in the evenings and the cruel comments of Fiona Bremner at school.

Fiona had started hassling him shortly after the accident. He hadn't remembered doing anything to start her off, but then Fiona never seemed to need a reason to pick on someone except a weakness. She never mentioned his dad's death but she constantly needled him about his lack of money, his old clothes and the things he didn't have.

Pete winced as he remembered some of her scathing remarks, always said in front of other kids for maximum effect.

Lines like, "Haven't you had that shirt since

junior school?" or "Those old trainers are years out of date."

Pete had tried to ignore her, but the more she went on, the more it got to him and he knew that it showed. That made it even worse.

As he started kicking the ball around with Tommy, Pete tried to push thoughts of Fiona out of his head. It was only later, when he was helping Tommy with his reading, that his mind drifted back to her spiteful taunts. He'd love to get even with her.

But little did he know then that doing so would spark off a series of events and send him down a path over which he had no control...

2

Revenge!

Pete was in a cheerful mood as he walked into school the next morning, but not for long. He'd only been in the building ten minutes before he was called into the Head's office. By the time he came out and headed into his History class he was in the blackest mood imaginable.

"Sorry I'm late Sir. I was..."

"I don't want to hear your excuses, Clark. Sit down." Mr. Baxter's gruff tones boomed through the classroom.

Pete slumped into his seat and brooded. He had wanted to explain. Being called to the Head's office wasn't a regular occurrence for Pete as it was for some kids. This was all about an anonymous note accusing Pete of stealing money from the school snack shop.

He hadn't taken the money – of course he hadn't – but the Head didn't seem convinced. Eventually she had dismissed him with the words, "All right, Peter. I'll believe you this time. Now, get back to class and buckle down. You can't afford not to, you know." Pete had shrugged his shoulders, desperately trying to look as though he didn't care.

"You can't afford not to." The words reverberated around his head as, angrily, Pete made his way out of History and into English. He knew he wasn't a genius – he'd always preferred sports to lessons – but he tried hard. That was more than could be said for that Fiona Bremner.

Pete stared out of the window as Mr. Robertson droned on about Shakespeare. Fiona must have sent the note. It was just the sort of thing she'd do. The more Pete thought about it, the more he was convinced, and the angrier he felt. He'd get her back... somehow.

There she was sitting two rows in front. He stared at her, his eyes boring into the back of her head, focusing all his anger and resentment. She was doodling on her notepad. He couldn't make out the letters but he could see a love heart drawn in red felt tip.

It was nearly the end of the lesson, when Mr. Robertson was called to the staff room, that Pete saw his chance. He got up from his desk and headed to the front.

"You've woken up then Pete?" said Graham

Johnson, the class joker. "Hey... what are you doing?"

Pete swept by Fiona's desk, grabbing her notebook. Ignoring her cries, he leapt to the front of the class. Pete stared at the notepad. There was the love heart. Inside was scrawled, *DJ 4 FB 4 Ever*. Without thinking twice about it, Pete shouted the message out to the class. Most of them laughed. Some glanced over to where Fiona sat. She looked straight ahead and didn't say a word.

"Who's DJ then?" piped up Graham Johnson. There were low murmurings around the classroom. "Aren't you going to tell us, Fiona?" he challenged. She didn't answer him.

Pete's mind raced, *DJ, DJ*. Of course... Pete plunged on.

"DJ, *darling* DJ is... Darren Jenkins," he announced coolly.

"What, Dazzer Jenkins in the year above!" one of the girls in the class exclaimed.

Pete looked over at Fiona. Her face was bright red, and he knew he'd hit the nail on the head.

"It's true. It's Darren Jenkins. Look at her," Pete cried. "She's blushing."

The whole class erupted into laughter and jeers.

"Fiona for Darren. Wait till I tell his mates," roared one of the boys.

"That's brilliant, Pete!" exclaimed Graham Johnson.

The bell rang and everyone began to troop out. First to the door was Fiona. For a brief second, Pete caught her glance. There were tears welling up in her eyes. Pete was surprised to feel a sudden stab of guilt, and quickly turned away.

In the playground at afternoon break, Jez raced over to Pete. "Heard about your English lesson today."

"What?" Pete began, surprised.

"It's all over the school," said Jez. "You're a bit of a hero. Fiona's a pain. She deserved it. You know she's gone home for the day?"

Pete shuffled his feet as he thought of her face. "I er... I think maybe I went too far."

"Nah, she had it coming to her," Jez smiled. "But I just hope you're ready for her brother."

"What? Big Stef? But he's not at school any more," Pete said quickly, but Jez had drifted off to swap game tips with the computer nerds from Class 3A.

Pete didn't actually know Fiona's older brother, Stefan, but he knew all about him. Big Stef was a bully, tough as you'd expect, but with a razor sharp mind as well. He knew exactly how to get what he wanted, how to touch kids' weak spots, even getting them to hand over their lunch money at the click of his fingers. Pete felt nervous just thinking about him.

At home time, Pete walked briskly through the school gates and began to make his way back to Ferndown Road, along the edge of the park. He found himself looking across the grass to the goal posts. Pete used to spend a lot of time down there, just kicking a ball around with his dad, but since he'd died, Pete hadn't felt much like being in the park. In fact, Pete had even stopped enjoying football so much. He tried to gee himself up for every game, especially for the really big ones, like the derby against local Telfer Heath and the grudge match against the snotty Oakmarsh Schoolboys with their fancy kit and full-time trainer. But somehow, without his dad on the sidelines bellowing his support, it just wasn't the same.

Pete was miles away in thought. Rounding a corner, he stopped dead. Straight ahead of him, a gang of lads, all dressed in black leather jackets, stood waiting. But it wasn't the number of them that caused Pete's heart to lurch. It wasn't even the way they bunched around him. It was the sight of the boy who strolled out from the back – the biggest of the lot. It couldn't be, could it? Pete swallowed hard. But there was no mistake. It was Fiona's brother, Big Stef, and he was heading straight for Pete.

3

The Chase

Stefan loomed over Pete. The smell of cigarette smoke on his breath was overpowering.

"Well, well, if it isn't Master Clark, curse of the schoolgirls," Stefan mocked. "Made my sister cry, eh? Looks like we've got ourselves a bully here lads."

The others laughed deep laughs. One of them cracked his knuckles. The sound made Pete wince.

"We don't like bullies, do we lads?" said Stefan, "Bullies must be punished. Isn't that right boys?"

"Yeah," chorused the gang. They started to circle Pete. He swallowed hard. He looked wildly around. There was no escape.

At that split-second, one of the thugs leaned against a parked car, setting off its alarm. Stefan's head turned in surprise. The timing was perfect. Now was Pete's chance. He made his break and sprinted down the road. With a huge bellow of "Get him!" from Stefan, the gang gave chase.

Looking behind him, Pete saw two of them unchaining their mountain bikes. He vaulted over a broken piece of park fence and raced across the grass.

Big mistake. His brain cursed his decision. The open ground was perfect for bikes. He heard the gang's whoops in the distance behind him.

Pete continued sprinting, his lungs pounding. There was someone on a bicycle in front of him. Someone he knew. It was Graham Johnson from school.

"Graham, Graham!" Pete called. "I need help. Can you give me a lift? QUICKLY!"

Perched precariously on the handlebars, Pete shut his eyes as Graham pedalled as hard as he could. Out through the other side of the park, Pete and Graham raced. The bike wobbled uncertainly and Graham had to swerve to avoid a couple of young kids. Pete glanced over his shoulder at the park. The bullies were a long way back.

Graham kept going for a couple more minutes before he looked behind. "Looks like we've lost them," Graham puffed, free-wheeling.

"No, keep going," Pete begged.

"All right," said Graham. "But only because you had the nerve to insult Fiona Bremner."

"That's why we're being chased," Pete replied.

"It's her brother."

Five minutes later, Graham drew to a halt. "That's it Pete. I've got to get back for my tea," he said in between huge gulps of air.

"Thanks Graham. I owe you."

Pete caught his breath as Graham pedalled away, and looked around. He was in unfamiliar territory. He wiped his sweaty forehead on his school pullover. Had they really cycled this far? He walked slowly down an empty street until he came to the entrance of a run-down old industrial estate. Pete glanced at the signpost... *Elmwood Enterprise Park*.

He didn't want to make his way home just yet. Maybe if he stayed out long enough, Stefan and his gang would grow tired of searching for him.

Pete walked into the industrial estate. The place seemed deserted. Most of the units were boarded up. As Pete turned the corner, a newer building came into view. It was painted black and on its side were the words *The Zone*. He ventured closer, his curiosity awakened. It was the only building he'd seen so far that seemed to be in use. He saw a couple of kids about his age walking out and another walking in.

Pete glanced at his watch. Whether he left for home now, or in half an hour, he was going to be late and get an earful from his mother. He might as well take a quick peep inside. Just a quick one, he told himself.

Leaning on the heavy steel and glass door and pushing it open, Pete stepped inside.

4

The Stranger in the Arcade

Two steps brought Pete up against some barriers. He leaned on them gently and they swung open like saloon doors in a Western.

It took some time for his eyes to adjust to the gloom. Inside was a video games arcade, but it was nothing like the one on the High Street which was brightly lit and always full of people.

Through the vast, dimly lit interior, he spied row upon row of arcade games. Only a few had players in front of them, their faces enveloped in the ghostly glow of the screens. There were lots of Street Stalker bash 'em up-type games, Grand Prix driving simulations and the usual Space Blaster consoles. But there were some he'd never heard of too – *Virtual Fighter*, *Memory Raider*, *Cubus*. Entering a second aisle of machines, Pete spotted a *Jinza* console. It was the arcade version of Jez's favourite computer game.

He'd never really been attracted to it on Jez's machine, but somehow here it looked as though it might be more exciting. Maybe he'd try it out. He fumbled around in his pockets for some change. Slipping a coin into the slot, he gripped the joystick. Scrolling through a choice of spacecraft, he waited patiently.

As the game started, Pete found himself at the helm of a spacecruiser darting through galaxies, blasting away against an enemy fleet. He tried to hide behind a small moon, but the ships pursued him, scoring a hit. Hammering the joystick's red trigger, Pete fought back. He blasted two of the enemy ships into smithereens, but when he tried to escape, his craft suddenly exploded into pieces. The screen went blank. Game over.

"Nice shooting."

The voice made him jump. Whirling around, Pete looked up to find a boy, much taller and a couple of years older, standing behind him. He had short blond hair and a stud in his left ear.

"What do you want?" Pete felt uneasy.

"Thought you might need a tip," the stranger said, scratching his crooked nose and then tucking his hand into the pocket of a worn leather jacket. "New here, aren't you?"

Pete nodded.

"Haven't been coming here long myself. Great

place, don't you think?" the strange figure went on.

"Er, yes," said Pete.

"About the tip. If they corner you, fire a smart bomb – yellow button on the back of the joystick."

Pete was a little spooked by the boy. He hadn't much liked the easy way he'd just started talking to him, or the idea that he'd been spying on him playing the game. He wanted to leave, he ought to leave, but he still had one credit. Stepping up to the console, he hit the start button again.

Racing through the first two levels, Pete found himself up against the four enemy ships again. This time, he managed to blast one out of the sky with a well-aimed laser missile. Pow! The other ships fought back. They bore down on Pete's vessel. Pete remembered the tip about the smart bomb just in time. He hit the yellow button. Kerboom! A huge, bright explosion filled the screen as Pete destroyed all three ships in one move.

He was onto the next level. Moments later, his ship was wrecked, but he didn't mind. That smart bomb tip would help when he next played Jez. He wanted another go, but he was out of money and anyway, he knew he should be getting back.

"Not going, are you?"

Pete turned around. It was the boy with the stud in his ear.

"Er, yes. Thanks for the tip. It really worked."

"I've got lots more? Want to see?" the boy asked.

Pete was unsure and remained silent.

"The name's Rick, by the way."

"I've got to get back," Pete mumbled.

"Come on, let me show you these tips." Rick pulled a handful of coins from his pocket and slipped a couple into the *Jinza* machine. "There we go. Two games to sharpen you up."

Pete hunched over the *Jinza* console as Rick stood at his shoulder, taking him through some fast moves. On the second game, Pete actually made it to a bonus screen. The game erupted into a series of bright flashes with a triumphant blast of sound. Pete felt a sudden surge of pride as a couple of players nearby turned around and looked at him.

The bonus level was phenomenally hard. Rick guided Pete past some of the hazards, but nothing prepared Pete for the five lightning-fast Battle Fighters now whizzing straight at him, their powerful laser cannons blazing.

"Hit them from right to left," Rick shouted.

Pete clamped his finger down on the joystick button and blasted away. He hit one battlefighter, but his aim was poor and he knew he'd missed the others. The screen cleared. That was it. All over. Then a few words flickered up.

> ## BONUS SCREEN COMPLETE
> ## FREE GAME   WELL DONE!!!

Pete was stunned. "Impossible... I'm sure I missed," he murmured.

"It looks like you didn't hit them," Rick replied, thumping the pause button. "But that's the key –

your brain and hands react faster than your eyes." Rick paused. "You're thinking and acting ahead of your senses. That's what makes you a natural."

"Really?" Pete was confused. He didn't believe he was really a natural – after all, he never even came close to Jez. Secretly though, he glowed at Rick's praise. Pete gave a quick glance at his watch.

"I really must be going now," he said.

"See you soon then?" Rick asked. "Tomorrow?"

"Maybe," Pete answered.

As Pete left the arcade, his eyes took time to adjust to the light outside. He'd explain to Mum about Stefan and the gang, but he didn't think he would mention *The Zone*. He wasn't quite sure why, but he suspected she wouldn't like the idea of him spending time in an arcade on the other side of town. If she didn't know, she couldn't tell him off.

Pete left *The Zone*, and headed off for home, not looking back. If he had, he may have seen a pair of eyes staring down at him from a small barred window. But he wouldn't have heard the strange, cruel laugh from behind the tiny, cracked window pane.

5

Back to *The Zone*

Pete leaned back in his chair, his hands laced behind his head. Jez looked at his friend in amazement. Pete was grinning broadly.

"I don't believe it," Jez gasped. "How did you do it? I had you cornered in the space hangars – you had no smart bombs left and only half power."

It was true. Pete had been about to lose his *Jinza* challenge with Jez until he remembered Rick's tips. After that, well, there could only be one winner.

Pete showed Jez the tips that Rick had taught him. Jez called them cheats. "And that gives you double thick shields?" Jez said, amazed.

Pete nodded and told him all about Rick and *The Zone*. "You've got to come. You'll love it."

"Okay, but you've changed your tune a bit

haven't you?" Jez grinned.

"Not really," Pete said defensively.

Since Pete had visited *The Zone*, he'd hardly been able to think about anything else. In any case, nothing else of interest had happened. School had been boring. Luckily, he hadn't bumped into Stef and his gang again. He'd thanked Graham for the bike ride and he'd made a special effort to steer well clear of Fiona Bremner.

On Saturday, Pete went back to *The Zone*. Jez had said he'd go with him, but had phoned the night before to say that his dad was taking him away for the weekend. Pete's mother had an afternoon shift so he had to be back for an early lunch. Still, he had a couple of hours.

Pete was surprised to find that *The Zone* wasn't much busier than before. Rick was there though. He led Pete over to a car racing game, *Monaco Madness*.

"Try it," said Rick. "It has fantastic gameplay." He pushed a coin into the slot. "I've got a great new tip for it."

Pete slid into the seat and played a couple of games. Rick was right. The graphics and the sound were excellent, but he just kept missing out on extra bonus laps.

Rick stopped him before his third game. "Here's a tip – tuck in behind the leader car on the long straight. Just as you approach the finish line, pull out and you'll find your car has tons more speed."

Pete started another game. Four laps later and

Pete had the race leader in his sights. As the finish line came into sight, Pete flipped his car out. Sure enough, just as Rick had said, his car zoomed past the leader.

A lap later, a computer voice blasted out of the machine. "New Lap Record," it screamed.

With his mind focused on the screen, Pete was hardly aware of the group that were crowding around him until one of them accidentally nudged him. His car had been approaching a tricky chicane and swerved off the track. A crash seemed certain and yet, suddenly there was his green racer back on the track. Pete was puzzled. Surely, he hadn't reacted in time, but he was still moving.

Lap after lap, Pete managed to keep going, always just getting a fast enough time to earn a bonus lap until ten laps later he hit a tight bend a fraction too fast. This time his car did crash. *Game Over*. Pete pulled himself out of the seat as the crowd gathered around him, congratulating him.

He felt proud. No one had praised him like that since he scored the winning goal against Oakmarsh School last year.

He looked around for Rick, but Rick hadn't been watching. Pete felt a sudden stab of disappointment as he spotted him on the other side of the arcade, hunched over a screen next to another kid. Pete decided to head home. As he got close to the exit, Rick called out. Pete pretended not to hear but Rick came racing over and flashed him a smile.

"How did you do?" he asked.

Pete shrugged his shoulders and continued walking towards the door.

"Come on, I'll show you an amazing game – not everyone's allowed to use it, you know."

"So why are you showing me?" asked Pete, warily.

"Because you're a natural," Rick replied. "Come on."

"I don't know," said Pete, wavering. "I don't get it. I don't play these games much. I don't even like them... I mean I didn't like them much. Now I'm getting all these high scores, and it's not just your tips."

"You said you like soccer, yeah?" said Rick, leading Pete over to the far side of the arcade.

Pete couldn't remember telling Rick that, but it was true so he nodded.

"Well, it's the same as that," said Rick. "There are players who look like they've made the wrong move but they haven't. In fact, they've made a move ahead of everyone else."

Pete understood. It was what Mr. Baxter, the school team coach, always droned on about.

"But I don't see how it applies to me," he added.

"The natural games player isn't some sad character who's always hanging around arcades, like those gamers," Rick explained, pointing at a few teenagers hunched over consoles. "The best players often don't realize they can be so good. And you know what sets them apart? Anticipation."

Pete laughed. Rick was serious though. Pete

avoided Rick's stare and looked around. Suddenly, he noticed an iron staircase leading up to an upstairs room.

"What's up there?" he asked.

"Up there? Oh that's the–" Rick paused, "that's the Inner Zone," he said as he walked on ahead.

Pete caught up. "The what?"

"The Inner Zone – it's Mr. Kagor's office and workshop," said Rick. "You're not allowed up there. No one is. Not without his permission."

"Who's Mr. Kagor?"

"He's the owner," Rick answered. "He designed some of these games himself. That's what he does up there."

"What? You mean he makes the games himself?" Pete was surprised.

"Something like that, but I don't know anything else, so don't ask," said Rick, suddenly defensive. Neither boy spoke as Rick led Pete to a roped off area on the far side of the building where a lone machine stood in a dark, empty corner. There was no one nearby.

"Should we be here? Are we allowed?" Pete asked nervously.

"It's fine. I've checked with upstairs. You're allowed."

"Upstairs? With Mr. Kagor? But I thought you weren't allowed..."

"It's fine," said Rick firmly. "This is *The Aggressor*," he said, pointing to the machine.

6

The *Aggressor*

Pete looked at the plain black console in front of him. It didn't look very impressive. If anything, it looked home-made. But it was expensive to play – double the price of other games in the arcade.

Following Rick's instructions, Pete picked up a shiny, black headset attached to the console. It was a Virtual Reality headset, just like the ones he'd seen on TV. He slipped it on. The headband and eyepieces were well padded and felt surprisingly comfortable.

Rick pointed to a pair of large black gloves wired up to the console. Gingerly Pete picked them up and slowly slipped his hands inside. The gloves felt warm and slightly moist but for some reason, it wasn't unpleasant. Pete felt his shoulders droop and his whole body relax.

"Do the straps up, but not too tight," Rick advised, putting in enough money for a game. "Now look around you."

Pete did as he was told. An array of images filled the headset. Up came an intro sequence together with some oriental-sounding music.

"It has a number of different games built in."

Pete could just make out Rick's voice over the sound of the machine.

"It picks one out at random," Rick went on. "What have you got?"

"Samurai Wars," Pete shouted.

The images slid away from Pete's view and in their place lay an empty Japanese-styled room. A length of bamboo cane lay on a straw mat in front of him.

"Can you see the fighting cane?" Rick asked. Pete nodded.

"Pick it up," said Rick.

"Don't be silly," Pete replied, screwing up his face.

"Go on. Move your hands forward and pick it up," said Rick.

Pete felt ridiculous as he stretched out towards the cane. Halfway towards it, he saw a pair of arms come into his field of vision, at the bottom. The arms were his. The left one even had his sports watch strapped onto its wrist, but they were cloaked in the billowing sleeves of some sort of white robe.

"Haven't you heard of Virtual Reality before?" Rick laughed.

"Course I have," Pete grunted.

Pete stretched his arms out further and closed his hands on the cane. Wow! He could actually feel it in his hands.

"How on earth?" gasped Pete.

"I don't know how they do it, but it's amazing, isn't it?"

Pete turned the cane over and over in his fingers. Was it really just a computer game?

"I'll tell you how to play," Rick announced. "Attack the warriors in black around the legs. The ones in blue are faster, but two or three strikes to the body will sort them out. The yellow bottles of potion give you extra strength. Got all that?" Rick sounded breathless.

Dazed, Pete nodded.

"Great. I've got to go now," said Rick. "Good luck."

Pete felt a little nervous. He wanted Rick to stay to help him, but somehow he felt he was in this game alone. It was all around him. He was a part of it.

Straight ahead of him he saw a large, slow-moving Japanese warrior. He shivered as the Samurai prowled around him.

The warrior's first strike seemed to hit Pete in the stomach. He didn't feel anything, but the speakers inside the headband registered a yelp of pain and he saw the counter showing his game strength drop by 10%.

Pete tried to defend himself by wielding the cane, but his attempts at attack were clumsy and he missed the black-robed warrior altogether.

The Samurai rapped his fighting stick hard. Pete marvelled at the shudder he felt through the gauntlets. This was incredible, so realistic. He was still marvelling at the effects when the warrior struck a combination of blows which ended the game. Suddenly the room disappeared and the view inside the headset went blank.

Before he could remove the headset and fumble around for some coins in his pocket, the game started up again all by itself.

Again he lost, but at least he caught the Samurai with one blow. Mysteriously, *The Aggressor* started a third game. This time Pete remembered Rick's advice and aimed at the black-robed warrior's legs. Pete took a lot of blows and his strength counter sank to just 20%, but a final crack across the Samurai's shins saw his opponent fall to the ground. Victory!

Pete was getting the hang of it. When the game ended next time, he had to put more money in. The same thing happened the time after. When he ran out of money, he finally removed the headset. He hadn't got past the first level, but he had improved and was pleased with his play.

Pete walked back through the arcade and looked around for Rick, but couldn't find him anywhere. As Pete left the building, he checked his watch. Half past twelve!

He'd been on *The Aggressor* for almost two hours. He'd completely lost track of time. How had he managed to play for so long? It hadn't felt that long. He'd only had to put money in the machine twice. Pete was puzzled, but by the time he got home, his mum was waiting in the hall for him.

"Where have you been, Peter? I asked you to be back by twelve. I've had to cancel my shift."

Pete thought about his answer. He never lied to his mum, but for some reason he thought it better not to tell her where he'd been.

"Sorry, I was out playing," he replied.

Before she could say any more, Pete nipped into the lounge and grabbed his little brother. "How about a kick around, Tommy?" He didn't really want to play with Tommy, but anything would do to avoid his mum for a short while.

Eagerly, Tommy raced out into the garden. Pete followed, passing his mum in the kitchen. She didn't say anything, she just sighed slightly.

Mrs. Taylor from next door frowned over her garden fence at Pete. "You mind that ball doesn't come into my garden," she called.

She turned away just in time to miss the face Tommy pulled at her. The two brothers started kicking the ball around but Pete's heart wasn't in it. His mind kept drifting back to *The Zone* and that amazing game. Somehow, kicking a ball around didn't seem much fun any more, not after real combat with Samurai warriors.

7

Meeting Mr. Kagor

Pete felt guilty, creeping out of the house the next morning before his mum and Tommy were awake. He left a note on the table, saying he was meeting a friend and would be back in time for lunch.

Tommy would be disappointed – they always took a ball out on Sunday mornings, but he'd make it up to him. He'd also make up the money he'd taken from Tommy's savings box. He could earn it back soon enough. He just wanted to make sure he had enough for a really long go on *The Aggressor*.

When he got to *The Zone*, it was already half full. But it felt different. The glow from the screens seemed unwelcoming, almost creepy. He didn't recognize any of the other players. There were none of the friendly faces from the day before, and there was no sign of Rick.

Suddenly he didn't feel comfortable about wandering over to the roped-off area where *The Aggressor* was, so he popped a coin into *Formula X*.

He gripped the wheel of his Grand Prix car as the starting grid flashed up on the screen. As Pete saw that he'd been placed sixth on the grid, a large, meaty hand clamped onto his shoulder.

"What do you think you're doing?" a voice asked.

"Just playing *Formula X*," Pete replied, pulling himself away from the hand. He looked up. A tall boy, older than Pete, towered over him. He was heftily built.

"I still had a credit left," the boy growled.

"You can't have..." Pete began.

"Are you calling me a liar as well as stealing my game?"

"No. I'm just saying that there honestly wasn't an extra game," Pete replied.

"I think there was," scowled the boy, angrily pulling off his baseball cap.

A computerized squeal of brakes and a crashing sound behind Pete told him that his game was over now. Pete felt annoyed. This thug had robbed him of his game. He was just about to say something when, out from the shadows, stepped two more well-built thugs. Pete looked anxiously from side to side, desperately hoping that Rick or one of the other regulars might have turned up. They hadn't. He was on his own.

"What's the problem?" came the voice of a third figure who strode out from the shadows. It was Stefan Bremner. Pete flinched.

"Didn't you know?" Stefan sneered, looking down at Pete, pinned against the console. "I'm head of security here." He pointed to a badge pinned to his shirt. "And you thought you'd escaped us, Pete Clark."

"But..." Pete started to protest, but he knew it was pointless. The three thugs and Stefan started closing in on him.

Then, out of the corner of his eye, Pete saw a movement from the top of the iron staircase. A door was opening. A man walked out onto the step and Stefan and his gang froze.

"It's Mr. Kagor," one of them gulped. The others just gawped.

Pete relaxed a little and turned to look at the man. He was thin with long black hair gathered into a ponytail. His clothes were scruffy – worn black jeans and an old jacket, but there was something very powerful about the way he stood there commanding absolute silence.

"What's the problem, boys?" Mr. Kagor asked at last.

His voice was much deeper and more resonant than Pete expected and his accent was strange, hard to place.

"It's this kid," Stefan said. "He's been causing trouble."

"No, I haven't," Pete protested. "I just came to

play a game."

"He took my credit," said the boy with the baseball cap. "He was–"

But before he had a chance to go on, Mr. Kagor put a finger to his lips and in an instant, Stefan's mates were silent.

"Go back to your duties, Stefan," said Mr. Kagor. "I'll speak with you later."

"Yes Mr. Kagor." Stefan Bremner nodded and sloped off back towards the machines.

"You," he pointed at Pete. "Come up here."

Pete's heart was pounding as he climbed the iron staircase until he was level with Mr. Kagor. The man was only a few inches taller than Pete but he didn't need height to exert his authority. His face was sharp and angular with rough grey stubble jutting from his chin. His eyes were a piercing light blue.

"What's your name?" Mr. Kagor asked.

"Pete. Peter Clark."

"Well, did you steal a credit, Peter?"

"No, Sir."

"This isn't school. You can call me Mr. Kagor."

"Yes, I mean no, Mr. Kagor."

Mr. Kagor almost smiled. "I've been observing you, Pete Clark. You're a promising games player, you know."

Pete felt himself blushing.

"Don't worry about Stefan and his friends. They're just some oafs I pay now and then to keep order and do odd jobs round the place. They get out of line sometimes. They won't bother you again."

Mr. Kagor paused. The silence seemed to hang in the air.

"I nearly forgot," he said, turning to leave. "Here's a present... to make up for the trouble. Spend them on *The Aggressor*. It's a challenging game, you know."

Mr. Kagor handed Pete a small plastic bag full of credit tokens for the games in the arcade. Pete dug his hand deep into the bag and pulled one out. There must have been 50 or 60 of them. Amazing! He looked up to thank Mr. Kagor, but he'd gone back into the gloom of his workshop.

Pete wandered around the arcade for a while. The incident with Stefan had unnerved him and part of him wanted to leave *The Zone*. Yet, another part of him was feeling very pleased, both with the free tokens and the compliments that Mr. Kagor had paid him.

Pete soon found himself in front of the strange black machine in the roped-off area again. He couldn't resist having a go.

He slipped on the machine's headset and gauntlets and placed four tokens in the slot. He was back in the Japanese room and ahead of him lay the cane, just waiting to be picked up. Pete grabbed it and waited until the Samurai warriors appeared. But after fighting them off for a few minutes, the headset blanked out. Pete cursed. He'd just been getting into it as well.

He began to unclip the headset when a new view

appeared. Bits of it looked familiar. He was standing in a grassy field – a cross between his school playing field and the park near his house. In the far distance something was moving towards him. As the objects got closer, the distant whine of motorbikes filtered through the speakers in the headset.

The whine became a deafening roar as the motorbikes got closer. Pete couldn't believe what he saw. *The Aggressor* had somehow created characters that he recognized... Stefan and his gang.

Pete looked down at his hands. The bamboo stick had turned into a pistol. For a moment, he was shocked. "It's okay," he told himself. "It's only a game."

He weighed the gun in his hand, he could even feel his finger's pressure on the trigger. It was incredible. Pete squeezed the trigger. His hand recoiled slightly as the pistol fired. His shot missed. The first thug on a motorbike was nearly upon him. Pete took aim again. Got him!

He turned to his left as another gang member appeared, a bicycle chain whirling around his head. Bang! Pete blew him off his saddle. The computer screen flashed 'Bonus Score' just as Stefan's image roared across the grass towards Pete. The video graphics were amazing. The computerized image of Stefan was incredibly accurate, right down to his ugly grin. Without flinching, Pete took careful aim and blasted Stefan off his bike. "Bonus Game," *The Aggressor* announced.

8

Mindreader

With the huge bag of tokens that Mr. Kagor had given him, Pete visited *The Zone* almost every evening during the following week. He dreaded another encounter with Stefan, but things seemed to have changed. Stefan was no longer any bother. He sometimes smiled tightly or coolly ignored him, but the big bully never hassled him again.

Every time Pete visited that week, Rick was there, always in his battered old leather jacket, whatever the weather.

"Aren't you hot in that thing?" Pete had asked one time as the two of them settled down for a game of *Virtual Fighter*. It was a hot day – the first real summer's day they'd had that year.

"Nah, not me," said Rick. "I always feel the cold.

35

Something to do with my ancestry."

Puzzled, Pete prompted Rick further.

"My mum came from Australia, married my dad and stayed, worse luck," he said, not looking up from the screen.

"Don't you like it here?" Pete asked.

"No I mean, worse luck she married my dad."

Rick's face was hard to read. Pete didn't pry any further. But a couple of days later, Pete couldn't resist asking more about Rick's family. "So they don't mind you spending all your time here then?"

"Who?" said Rick.

"Your parents."

"They don't know. I don't live with them any more." Rick turned away as he spoke.

"Where *do* you live then?" Pete asked.

"Oh, not far away." Rick's features tightened into a fierce frown. Pete didn't ask any more questions after that.

Pete always played the odd game or two with Rick, but gradually he found himself spending more and more time alone on *The Aggressor*. The machine seemed to be increasingly challenging each time he played it. Pete was amazed at the range of foes he encountered. Sometimes there were Samurai warriors, other times Roman soldiers, Western outlaws, even American gangsters. But it was the personal bits that made Pete come back to the game again and again.

How could a machine know how much he disliked his next door neighbour, Mrs. Taylor, or that he was feeling hassled by the football coach, Mr. Baxter? But it did. *The Aggressor* gave Pete fantastic opportunities to vent his frustration.

While Pete was quite happy to ask Rick for his advice on other machines, he never wanted to ask Rick for help on *The Aggressor*. He felt the game was his and only he could solve it or win through to a new level. After a week or two, he had almost stopped playing any of the other machines at *The Zone*.

And the more time he spent at *The Zone*, the less time he spent on other things – school, friends, even Tommy. He knew he'd been neglecting his brother lately. He still kicked a ball around with him – when he had to – but he did it half-heartedly. His mum had started being a real pain as well – asking him to help out more and more, and then moaning when he didn't have the time to do it.

Thursday night, exactly three weeks and one day after Pete's very first visit to *The Zone*, Pete was helping his younger brother with his reading cards. His mood got worse and worse and he lost his temper.

"A-N-D spells AND. We've been doing these same cards for weeks," Pete snapped.

Tommy hung his head and looked blank.

"Oh, there's no point in me helping you," Pete exploded. "You're too thick."

Tommy didn't say anything, but Pete saw he was upset.

"Hate reading anyway," Tommy shouted,

slamming the door and running to his room. Pete knew he ought to go up and say sorry, do something. But he didn't. He blocked out the sound of Tommy in his bedroom upstairs and sat on his own in the lounge, doing nothing, just feeling miserable and quiet and terribly lonely.

He wasn't feeling much better at school the next day. It must have been obvious, because Graham Johnson came up to him after Geography.

"You all right, Pete?" he asked.

"I'm fine," Pete replied firmly, irritated by Graham interfering.

"Everyone's noticed how quiet you are these days."

"Let them notice," Pete muttered.

"You know Fiona's theory about you?" said Graham.

"No," Pete replied sharply.

"She's been bragging that her brother beat you up and now you're scared." Graham waited for a response, but Pete was silent.

"But we know you got away, eh?" Graham winked. Pete flinched inside. Who did Johnson think he was, treating him like he was his best mate?

Pete shrugged his shoulders. It hadn't taken long for Fiona Bremner to start needling him again. But he wasn't about to admit that to Graham Johnson. He walked off, trying hard to look as if he didn't care. But he was still brooding over things when Jez caught up with him at the end of school that day.

"Hello, it's er, what's your name again?" Jez began in a falsely cheerful voice. "Didn't I use to know you?"

Pete spun around. He hadn't been to Jez's house for ages. He'd been too busy, what with going to *The Zone* whenever he could.

"Very funny, Jez," said Pete.

"I'm free this Sunday," said Jez, still in his chirpy tone. "I thought we could go to that arcade of yours."

Suddenly Pete's mood brightened. He'd show Jez just what he'd been missing for the past few weeks.

"All right," said Pete. "I'll call for you at nine on Sunday then."

"Nine! That's early." Jez looked dismayed.

"Ah but you need to be there early to get on *The Aggressor*," said Pete. "It's the best machine."

"Okay then, I'll be up in time." Jez shrugged his shoulders.

* * * * * * * * * * * * * *

Pete went back to *The Zone* that evening with just enough money for a couple of plays.

The Aggressor started in typical fashion with Pete cutting and blasting his way through swathes of Samurai warriors. Then the game took an unexpected twist. He found himself as one of a team of bank robbers escaping from the scene of a crime. Pete's hand in the Virtual Reality glove was carrying a big bag, full of money.

It took Pete a while to listen to the soundtrack thumping through the speakers in the headset. There was typical-sounding chase music interrupted by explosions and guns firing. And yet, there was also something else.

Part of the soundtrack seemed to be his mum's voice. Pete stopped for a moment. He must be imagining things, he thought. He listened again, only harder. This time her voice was clear and unmistakable. "You can't just throw your money away, Peter. Money doesn't grow on trees you know." She repeated the words over and over. Pete marvelled at *The Aggressor*. Those were just the words Mum would have used. Pete felt a sudden stab of guilt.

The screen cleared and Pete pushed the uncomfortable thoughts of his mother to the back of his mind. There was a new scene in front of his eyes. The bag of cash in his hand had been replaced by a revolver. Pete could feel the lighter weight of the gun through the gauntlet's pressure pads.

Now the view changed. The streets faded into the hallway of a small house. He looked at his feet standing on a familiar wooden floor. Pete turned his head. Yes, there was the old umbrella stand in the corner. It was the hall of his own house in Ferndown Road.

Pete began to walk slowly down the hallway. Ahead in the kitchen, he could hear the sound of food frying. Slowly, he opened the door to find three men with knives.

It no longer felt like a game. Pete was scared, but he couldn't stop. He had to carry on. Every muscle in his arms was taut as he prepared to attack the intruders. The fight was fast and furious, he was no match for these men and their knives. Then he remembered the gun and fired. Two figures slumped to the floor, but one remained. A big, hulking gangster in a hooded coat and dark glasses was coming straight at him, knife in hand. Pete edged back and began raising his hands as if in surrender. No. Stop. What was he doing? He lifted the gun and pulled the trigger at point blank range.

Minutes later, Pete was running from *The Zone*, tears in his eyes. For when he had looked closer at the final figure he'd gunned down, he saw that the hood had slipped back and the glasses had fallen off to reveal a computer-simulation of someone very familiar. It was his dad.

That night, back at home with the rest of his family asleep, the nightmares began...

9

Nightmares

Trapped in a corner with nowhere to run, the brightest of lights tore into his eyes. He tried to shield himself from the glare but couldn't. In front of him, he could make out who it was... Fiona Bremner, but she was twice her normal height. Looking closer, her left arm was made of metal. It glinted wickedly under the harsh light.

"You must pay," Fiona spat.

"What for?" Pete wanted to ask. He opened his mouth, but the words wouldn't come. Fiona smiled evilly over him.

"You've got to pay the price, Pete Clark. You've got to pay for what you've done."

A strange whirring sound filled his ears. He looked in horror at Fiona's robot limb. At the end was a horrific collection of wickedly curved metal blades, spinning violently.

She leant towards him, the blades looming ever closer as the whirring sound grew to a crescendo.

"You've got to pay. You've got to pay." Louder and louder, again and again. He screamed.

Pete woke up bathed in sweat, his heart pounding. He glanced at his clock, it was only 4:30. He wiped his matted fringe back from his forehead and took deep breaths. He'd had bad dreams before, especially when he was younger, but this was different, more real, much more terrifying.

"Mum! MUM!" he screamed.

The door burst open.

"What's wrong?" Pete's mum asked in alarm.

"I've just had a terrible nightmare," he cried.

"Is that all? I thought you'd hurt yourself."

"It was terrible, Mum. There was this..."

Pete tried to explain, but his mum cut him short.

"Peter, just go back to sleep. I'm tired. I've got a double shift today. I need my sleep and I can't cope with you waking me in the middle of the night. You're worse than Tommy."

"But Mum..."

"But, nothing. When you do what you're asked to do and start acting your age, you won't have nightmares." She shut the bedroom door firmly.

Pete lay awake in the dark for ages, watching the fluorescent numbers on his alarm clock. He didn't feel so scared any more, but he felt alone... terribly alone. Then, just as the daylight began to

43

creep through the cracks in his curtains, he fell into an uneasy sleep. When he next looked over at his alarm clock, he cursed. 9:55. He was supposed to meet Jez at nine o'clock sharp.

Pete forgot all about his nightmare as he leapt out of bed and got dressed. He hadn't seen much of Jez at school or in the evenings. He was excited to be taking him to *The Zone* at last.

Pete crept into the kitchen. Standing on tiptoe, he reached up for his savings box on top of the kitchen cupboard. He carefully pulled out some money. Not much left.

By the time Pete reached Jez's flat, it was nearly half past ten.

"Oh very funny, Clark," Jez muttered. "I've been waiting for hours."

"I'm sorry," said Pete.

The pair walked in silence through the park.

Pete led Jez through the zigzagging streets and into the industrial estate. Jez seemed uneasy as they walked along the empty road, past the deserted buildings.

"You sure it's safe over here?"

"Of course it is, especially if you're with me," Pete swaggered.

"Oh excuse me, tough guy," Jez retorted sarcastically.

Jez perked up when he spied *The Zone*.

"It's certainly big enough," said Jez appreciatively.

"Of course it is," replied Pete, pushing open the

doors without a moment's hesitation.

Jez followed uncertainly, casting his eyes this way and that as they wandered through the gloom. Pete traded quick nods with a couple of gamers hunched in front of machines.

"You actually like it here?" Jez muttered incredulously.

Pete looked back at him, puzzled. He was used to the gloom and found himself mildly irritated by Jez's anxiousness.

"So where's this wonder game you were talking about?" Jez asked.

"It's over here, come on," said Pete, marching Jez to the roped off corner of the room. Proudly, Pete pointed to the machine.

"What's this heap of junk?" Jez asked.

"It's *The Aggressor*," Pete replied defensively. "The best game here."

"More like someone's failed computer project. Look at all this loose wiring," said Jez.

Pete ignored him.

"Have you seen how much this costs?" Jez said in alarm. "It's double all the others."

"It's worth it," replied Pete impatiently.

"I don't know Pete, I'd rather have a couple of games of *Virtual Fighter* or *Street Stalker* than blow all my money on this heap."

"It isn't a heap," Pete snapped angrily.

"Okay, okay. If you're getting so worked up about it, it must be good."

Pete watched as gingerly Jez slipped the headset

on and put his money into the slot. "Looks like your standard Virtual Reality stuff," he mumbled.

"Get on with it," Pete growled.

By the time Jez started the game, Pete felt really irritated by his friend's behaviour. From the moment he'd met him, and all the way here, Jez had been moaning about this and that, doubting every word that Pete had said. He just can't bear me finding a game he's never played, Pete thought to himself.

Pete watched as Jez played *The Aggressor*. By the way his hand and head ducked and dived about, it seemed to be a furious bit of gameplay. Pete sniggered at his friend's yelps and cries. Wearing the headset and gauntlets, Jez did look silly.

Two minutes later, dazed and glassy-eyed, Jez stepped out of the console. Pete looked at him, his excitement mounting. Jez was slow to speak.

Pete could barely contain himself any longer.

"Well, what do you think?" he asked.

Jez didn't say a thing.

Pete saw his friend trembling. "Hang on, I know it's a bit freaky at first, but it's an amazing game, eh, Jez... Jez?"

But Jez wasn't listening, he was already halfway out of the arcade.

"I'm going Pete. Don't ever ask me to play that game again."

Angrily, Pete chased Jez and caught up with him. Dazzled by the bright sunlight, both boys were silent for a moment.

Jez turned to him.

"Sorry Pete, but that really scared me." He gave a weak grin.

"What's wrong with you?" Pete exploded. "Don't you know how uncool it is to run out of an arcade. I mean, what are the other gamers going to think? I bring you in here and..."

"I'm going," Jez interrupted firmly.

In a foul mood, Pete turned back to *The Zone*. Half an hour on *The Aggressor*, shooting down legions of World War One fighter planes, all piloted by a figure that looked like Jez, made him feel better.

But the great feeling didn't last long. When he left *The Zone* to make the long walk back to Ferndown Road, he felt even worse than before.

10

Confrontation

The next day, back at school, things didn't start too well for Pete. But it wasn't anything to do with Jez or even Fiona Bremner. It was more to do with the telling-off he got in Science, followed by the lecture from Mr. Baxter for missing football training.

"I don't know what you're thinking about Clark, the trials for the summer tour are three days away."

"Three days!" Pete was surprised. He'd lost all track of time recently.

"Yes, laddie. And those that are picked, get a cheap holiday as well as a free new kit. But then, you would have known all about that if you'd been to training recently."

"Yes Sir, sorry."

Pete found it hard to concentrate all through his next class. As he left the Art room, he heard his name called from down the corridor in strong tones. It was Mr. Robertson, the English teacher.

"What have I done wrong now, Sir?" Pete asked wearily.

"Nothing lad, nothing at all." Mr. Robertson seemed surprised. "I was just going to say, if you ever need a chat about anything..." His voice tailed off and he stared at Pete for a short while before walking away.

School seemed to be passing more slowly and painfully than it ever used to. Pete found it almost impossible to concentrate and received lecture after lecture for not paying attention, as well as for his poor work in class and at home.

He also found himself getting riled at the smallest thing. He now shoved younger kids when they jostled him in the lunch queue when in the past, they wouldn't even have bothered him. And the other day he nearly walked out of class when a student teacher forgot his name.

"It's Paul isn't it?"

"No, it's Pete," he'd said in an aggressive voice.

"Of course, Pete Duncan," the teacher began.

"Clark," said Pete, staring straight at the teacher. "C-L-A-R-K." He spelt it out feeling ready to explode as some of his classmates had giggled behind him. If only everyone at school could see me at *The Zone*, he thought bitterly. They wouldn't laugh then.

49

Pete bumped into Jez in the playground on the day before the soccer trials. He hadn't seen him since their argument at the arcade. He guessed he should say sorry or something.

Jez eyed him cautiously.

"Er, sorry about before, Jez. I was a bit uptight."

"You're telling me. What's wrong Pete?"

"Nothing's wrong with me," Pete bristled.

"Well, why don't you come round tomorrow? That's if you can spare the time," Jez joked.

"I can't. I'm going to *The Zone*," Pete replied testily. "You could come too if you weren't too scared."

"To that arcade? No way," Jez said dismissively. Pete felt his irritation increase.

"I'm going," he said.

"Fine, well I'll see you when you're better."

"Better? What do you mean?" Pete growled.

"Well there's obviously something wrong with you. Graham Johnson says..."

Pete cut him off. "Graham Johnson's an idiot."

"Oh really? A couple of weeks ago, he was the friend who saved you from Big Stef. See, there is something wrong with you," he said.

The hairs on the back of Pete's neck started prickling and he felt a hot angry flush rise through him.

"What's wrong with *me*? What's wrong with *you*,

spotty?"

Pete had never mentioned his friend's spots before.

"What did you call me?" It was Jez's turn to rage.

"I called you spotty, acne-face, pizza features, is that clear enough for you?" Pete sneered.

"Clear enough that you're mental, Clark," Jez shouted back.

Pete lunged forward, furious.

Jez retaliated.

In the five years they'd known each other, Jez and Pete had never traded blows. Both were surprised by the ferocity of each other's attack and it took a couple of boys to separate the warring friends. It was lucky for both of them that there wasn't a teacher around.

* * * * * * * * * * * * * * *

Later on, Pete met Rick at the entrance to *The Zone*.

He was standing there, hands in the pocket of his old jacket, shoulders hunched. "How are you doing?" Playfully Rick punched Pete's arm. Pete stepped away rapidly.

"Fine," Pete said quietly. "Just fine."

"What's wrong?" Rick asked, concern showing in the furrows on his forehead.

"Everyone's always asking me what's wrong.

Nothing's wrong," Pete shouted.

"Okay, okay. Sorry I asked."

"I punched my best mate, that's all." Pete blurted it out. Rick was silent. The two of them walked into the arcade, not saying a word.

Pete didn't get home until long after it was dark that evening. After *The Aggressor* had been switched off and *The Zone* had been shut, he had wandered aimlessly around the industrial estate, deep in thought.

He'd played game after game on *The Aggressor* that day. Each time, faces of people he knew mixed with anonymous villains. At first he'd managed to vent his rage on lots of figures that all looked like Jez. Yet, after each game, Pete had felt more and more angry. This bothered him. When he'd first played *The Aggressor*, the machine had calmed him down. Now, it seemed to pump him up, made him angry, violent even. He'd gone to *The Zone* hoping it would make him feel better after his terrible day at school. Now he felt worse.

"Where have you been?" his mum demanded when eventually he got in. She was in almost as bad a mood as Pete. "I've managed to get an evening shift. Can you look after Tommy?" she asked curtly.

"Can't he look after himself?" Pete asked equally brusquely.

"Of course he can't Pete," said his mum. "He's six. What do you think? Look, this has been hard for all of us, I know, but we've got to try and pull through as a family. This shift is double-time. Extra money. We need it. We've all got to make sacrifices."

"What do you know about sacrifices?" Pete shouted.

Mrs. Clark opened her mouth. Pete thought she was about to yell at him, but she didn't. "I can't deal with this now, Pete," she said, tight lipped. "I'll talk to you later." She slammed the front door behind her.

"Where's Mum gone?" Tommy was sitting at the top of the stairs in his pyjamas.

"Out," Pete snarled. "Now shut up and go to bed."

"Don't want to. I want Mummy." Tommy's eyes began to well up with tears.

"Well, you can't have her," Pete said cruelly. "Now push off you cry baby," he roared.

For the rest of the evening, Pete's brain didn't even register the muffled sounds of his brother crying upstairs. Pete was elsewhere, feeling angry, thinking about his dad and his fight with Jez, but most of all, about *The Aggressor*.

11

On Trial

Pete felt a surprise burst of confidence when he came down the stairs the next morning. Tommy and his mum had already left, but on the table he found the good luck note they had left him for the football trials – not that he'd need it of course, after all, he was one of the key players on the team. Sure, he hadn't been to training lately, but that shouldn't prove to be too much of a problem.

By the time school ended, Pete was feeling more confident than ever. He felt much more aggressive and that had always been Mr. Baxter's complaint about him – Pete was a skilful player but he didn't always 'get stuck in enough'.

Two hours later, after Mr. Baxter blew the whistle and Pete headed off for the showers, he felt proud of himself. He'd enjoyed the game. He knew he'd missed a couple of tackles, and he should have put away that open goal, but he thought he'd had a good game.

Pete was surprised to be called into Mr. Baxter's office after showering. Surely he hadn't been good enough to be given the captaincy, he thought. As he entered Mr. Baxter's cramped room, he pulled his shoulders back proudly.

"You wanted to see me, Sir?" he said.

"Yes Peter." Mr. Baxter was fiddling with a boot stud remover. "I'll come straight to the point. You're out of form. I don't know what's wrong with you, missing all those training sessions and looking so unfit on the pitch, but if you knuckle down, you'll get your place back after the tour."

"Get my place *back*?" Pete couldn't believe what he was hearing. He stared at Mr. Baxter. The coach wasn't joking. He had been dropped!

Pete could feel the fury exploding inside his head. "You can stick your stupid team," he shouted, slamming the office door. Anger and resentment burned fiercely within him. He was beside himself with rage. "How dare he. How dare he!" Pete cried out, stomping down the corridor, his muddy boots slung over his shoulder.

As he turned into the main corridor leading out of the building, a fire alarm button protected by a square pane of glass, caught his eye.

For a moment he stopped. A tiny flicker of calm wavered inside him, but he disregarded it and with a flourish, flung one of his boots at the glass of the fire alarm, and raced out of the school.

His mind still filled with fury, Pete ran as hard as he could through the maze of streets that led to the industrial estate. But as he reached *The Zone*, he cursed. It looked closed. It wasn't that late, but he should have remembered it sometimes shut early during the week. He leaned on the door, just in case, and to his surprise found it still open. He walked inside.

All the lights were off, except for the ones in the room upstairs. Pete crept to the bottom of the stairs. What did Mr. Kagor do up there that kept him in his workshop all of the time?

The eerie silence was suddenly broken by two angry voices upstairs.

"I've had enough. You owe me. If you don't pay up, I'm going to the police."

"You wouldn't dare. I already overpay you as it is."

"I know what you're up to here with that *Mindmaster* machine you're so proud of nearly finishing. I've seen too much for you not to pay me."

"I suppose it serves me right for getting a kid to do a man's job. You walk out now and you'll be in more trouble than you could possibly imagine." The voice was Mr. Kagor's.

"Yeah, well you don't scare me. I guess I'll have to take my chances."

The door suddenly burst open, almost off its

hinges, and Stefan stormed out, looking angrier than Pete had ever seen anyone look. Quickly Pete ducked under the iron staircase, out of sight.

As the door to the upstairs room slammed shut, Stefan's boots went thumping over Pete's head, down the steps and away out of the building. Taking a deep breath, and keeping a safe distance behind, Pete followed him.

Peering around the corner of the swing doors, Pete watched Stefan throw something into a yellow skip nearby. Pete waited until Stefan had grabbed his bike and pedalled off in a rage. Pete looked around to make sure no one was watching, crept over to the skip and peered in.

It was full of builders' debris, rubble and broken bricks, twisted coils of steel cable, and smashed slates. But Pete was intrigued and he pulled himself up into the skip. Moving a rotted window frame aside, he spotted Stefan's security badge. Right next to it was a small red notebook. Stefan must have thrown that away with the badge, Pete thought, blowing the brick dust off of its cover. Opening it up, he found it full of a thin spidery scrawl which was hard to decipher. He scrunched up his face and squinted hard at the neatly ruled pages, gradually working out what it said.

The first part of the notebook was full of cheats for the latest arcade games. There was one for *Street Stalker* and one for *Monaco Madness* – in fact, they were all for games at *The Zone*.

There were a couple of empty pages, then a page

with a single line which read *Mindmaster: never cross the void*.

The back section of the notebook looked like a coded message; rows of numbers and letters that didn't make any sense. Perhaps it was a computer program, though he couldn't imagine Stefan being an accomplished computer boffin.

Pete ducked down out of sight as he heard the front door of the arcade being opened. He kept low as he listened to the sound of keys being used, then footsteps and a motorbike starting. When the roar of the bike had died away, Pete hopped out of the skip and walked out of the industrial estate.

When he eventually got home, he found himself in huge trouble with his mother. Mr. Baxter had phoned her about the fire alarm business and she was furious.

At the end of the yelling, Pete stormed out into the garden. Nosy Mrs. Taylor was staring out of her kitchen window at him. He stared hard back at her until she disappeared behind her net curtains. Pete turned away and took a swiping kick at Tommy's ball lying on the path. Pete's eyes followed the ball to the end of the garden, to the far corner where the old greenhouse... It was gone. Dad's old greenhouse had disappeared leaving a rectangular patch of concrete where it had stood. The panes of glass stood neatly stacked against the fence.

Pete reeled. He felt another hot wave of anger flood through him.

"Where's the greenhouse?" he yelled through the

back door.

"Someone at work got rid of it for me," his mum said, walking out into the garden. "It was falling down. There was no point having it fixed, even if we'd had the money – no one but your father used it. Now let's have some supper. I've got some of those special burgers you love in the freezer. We could have them in buns."

"Shut up. Shut up about stupid burgers. What about the greenhouse!" Pete exploded. "It was Dad's greenhouse, how could you get rid of it?"

Pete felt like a huge weight was bearing down on him. It hurt and he wanted to cry, only he couldn't.

His mum tried to comfort him and went to put an arm on his shoulder but Pete pulled away.

"Leave me alone!" he cried.

12

The Cheats

Pete went to bed early that night. He felt so angry and frustrated that it took him a while to fall asleep. And when he did sleep, he dreamed of broken buildings, piles of bricks and rubble. He seemed to be searching for something, hunting through the wreckage for something he'd lost. And all the while, he felt that he was being watched... watched by some invisible eye.

When he woke, he was alone in the house. His mum had already taken Tommy off early for a special class with his remedial teacher. With no one to yell at him to get a move on, Pete lingered in the kitchen, eating a bowlful of cereal. Then he took his time getting washed and dressed before he finally left the house, much later than usual.

Looking at his watch, he knew he'd already missed assembly and was late for his first lesson.

Stepping through the school gates, he decided he couldn't face going any further. In fact, there was only one place he felt like going. Pete set off to *The Zone*, ignoring the pangs of guilt that stabbed at his conscience.

Rick wasn't around. Funny... Pete thought he would be. Maybe Rick did go to school after all. Pete didn't recognize any of the other players there and his mood turned sour and jealous as he saw someone else using *The Aggressor* machine.

"Hope he's got permission," Pete muttered.

Pete had copied out the cheat for *Cubus* from the notebook.

Level 4: stay hard left of the 2nd platform = extra lives

Pete hurried over to where the machine was lying in a deserted aisle. Soon Pete was battling through the first three levels with relative ease. He had to get *Cubus* up the screen without being splashed by any of the acid rain waterfalls or jumped on by the enemy, the patrolling Green Meanies.

Quickly he moved *Cubus* up to the second platform and tugged the joystick left. *Cubus* struggled, but Pete kept him hard up against the edge of the screen. Along the platform tramped a legion of Green Meanies ready to pounce.

Pete thought twice, but kept *Cubus* in position. As the Meanies hit, something strange happened.

61

As each Meanie jumped on *Cubus*, the game lives counter went up instead of down. By the time all of the Meanies had attacked, the counter had rocketed to 19 lives. Fantastic!

With so many lives at his disposal, Pete was able to navigate the next half a dozen levels with ease. Twice he even sacrificed a life just to avoid having to play a tricky part of the screen.

As level 12 appeared, loud music blasted out of the arcade speakers. The sound attracted the attention of some of the other players and soon there was a crowd behind him.

"How's it going?" one of the gamers asked, "Level 12, eh? Cool."

"Shh, leave me alone," Pete snapped. He felt the pressure now. He wanted to perform well in front of everyone. Dragging the joystick hard to the right and pressing the turbo jump button, he managed to get *Cubus* clear of a rolling ball of fire. He was very close to level 13 now. He remembered Rick saying once that no one at *The Zone* had ever reached level 13.

"You're wanted upstairs," a voice echoed through the crowd. "Mr. Kagor wants to see you."

"What me? Mr. Kagor?" Pete shouted, suddenly losing concentration over the crowd's murmurings.

"Yes and he said immediately," the voice replied.

Pete's shoulders dropped. He'd have to try for level 13 another time.

Pete left the machine and pushed his way through the throng of disappointed gamers. Slowly and nervously, he climbed the iron staircase up to the door. Rick had managed to make the Inner Zone sound daunting. He reached the door. He thought about turning back. Instead, he leant on the handle and went inside.

13

Virtual Addiction

"Nice to meet you again." Mr. Kagor wiped his hands on his black jeans and adjusted his black leather waistcoat, before thrusting out his hand and leading Pete into the middle of his workshop.

Is this it? Is this the Inner Zone? Pete looked around feeling slightly disappointed. The large room was lit by a naked light bulb and shafts of light from a small barred window and a skylight in the roof. Through the gloom, he saw a mess of computers and electronic parts. There was a filing cabinet, two large desks and a computer terminal linked to what looked like three or four powerful games machines. Printers on the far side of the room were churning out page after page of continuous

64

paper.

"I like to talk to my more loyal customers," Mr. Kagor said in his curious, deep voice. "You are a loyal customer aren't you?" Pete nodded his head.

"You don't visit other arcades now, do you?"

Pete shook his head.

"Good, and everything that you need is here?"

"Yes."

"I've seen you play *The Aggressor* lots of times. What do you think of it?" Mr. Kagor played with his ponytail absent-mindedly.

"It's amazing."

"It's meant to be," Mr. Kagor smiled.

"How does it work?" Pete began. "I mean how does it know what I'm thinking, how does it take my thoughts... my memories and use them like it does?"

"Oh, it doesn't *take* memories. *The Aggressor* just uses your thoughts while you're playing the game. It only *borrows* them to make the game more interesting."

"Borrows?" Pete asked, surprised at the stress Mr. Kagor put on the word.

"Yes," said Mr. Kagor, without expression. "We're generous, we give them back."

"Well, you can't really take them can you?" said Pete. "Well, not forever."

"Who knows?" said Mr. Kagor.

Pete was feeling puzzled, uncertain why he was having this strange conversation and uncertain where it was leading. Mr. Kagor was looking at the open door on the far side of the workshop. Pete followed his gaze in the direction of an open doorway. He could see a bare room with a white sheet draped over a bulky shape.

"What's that?" asked Pete, changing the subject and pointing to it.

"Oh, that," Mr. Kagor replied, "That's just a new games machine I'm developing."

"What's it called?"

"*Mindmaster*," Mr. Kagor answered abruptly, walking over and slamming the door shut. "It's called *Mindmaster*, but I didn't ask you up here to talk about that. I wanted to talk about *you*. You're having trouble at school aren't you?"

Pete's heart skipped a couple of beats. Caught in his icy blue stare, Pete felt compelled to tell Mr. Kagor the truth about what had been going on at school. The only thing he didn't mention was the punch up he'd had with Jez. Pete felt too ashamed to tell Mr. Kagor about fighting with his friend. When he'd finished, Mr. Kagor looked thoughtful for a moment.

"You've been thumping your friend, Jez, recently, haven't you?" said Mr. Kagor.

"How do you know?" Pete was surprised and slightly shocked.

"I know a lot about you, Pete Clark. I know that you were in a car accident with your father. You weren't scratched but your father died. I know you have a little brother called Tommy and a mother who's working at lots of different jobs to make ends

66

meet."

"How do you know all this?" he gasped, thinking hard. "Rick. It must be Rick!" Pete cried out loud. "He's the only one who knows all that. But I told him in confidence."

"Rick tells me everything," said Mr. Kagor with a slight thin-lipped smile. *"He has to."*

Pete looked shocked.

"I thought you would have realized that by now," said Mr. Kagor. "I give him free run of the arcade. In return, he makes friends with new visitors and gets them to come back. It's probably best for someone like you to steer clear of him."

"What do you mean?" Pete stammered.

"Well, he can't be trusted. He lies to people and steals things, just so that he can get to play more and more video games. He's hooked you see – an addict. What you might call a Virtual Addict." Mr. Kagor laughed, as if he'd made a joke. "He can't leave the machines alone. It's tragic really."

Pete wrestled with this news about Rick as Mr. Kagor leaned back on his cluttered workbench and spoke again. "How did you manage to do so well on *Cubus*, Pete?"

Pete's mind raced for a couple of seconds. What should he say? He didn't want to admit to taking the notebook out of the skip. Mr. Kagor would be sure to put two and two together and realize he'd overheard the argument.

"Someone from school gave me some tips," Pete lied.

Mr. Kagor looked hard at him. As Pete began to squirm under Mr. Kagor's laser-like stare, the phone rang. He picked it up and muttered briefly.

"Uh huh... the components I ordered. Yes. Good. But I need them tomorrow. No... they haven't got any serial numbers, have they? Good. Yes, payment as agreed."

Mr. Kagor turned to Pete. His expression was hard to read, but much to Pete's relief, he seemed to have forgotten his last question.

"There's one thing I'd like you to do for me, Pete," Mr. Kagor began. "Stefan and I had a disagreement – nothing serious, but he's taken something that belongs to me and I'd like it back. If you see him, perhaps you could tell him to come and see me. Tell him I want to make things up with him."

Pete nodded and forced a smile. If the disagreement was the one he'd heard, 'nothing serious' didn't seem the right description for it.

"Don't look so worried," said Mr. Kagor in a smooth voice. "Tell you what, I'll give you the ultimate gaming tip for *The Aggressor*."

Mr. Kagor stood close to Pete, his eyes fixed firmly on him. Caught in Mr. Kagor's gaze, Pete listened as if his life depended on it.

"To merge yourself with the machine, to make yourself the perfect match to the machine's abilities – that's the ultimate aim. You need your head – your skull – as close to the sensors inside the headset as possible. Any gap between brain and machine can make all the difference. It could be all that's standing between you and the highest levels of *The Aggressor*."

Mr. Kagor handed Pete another bag of arcade game tokens. "With Stefan gone, I need loyal players who can be trusted. Enjoy, my friend."

"Thank you Mr. Kagor," Pete replied.

His head was buzzing. Despite being upset about Rick and the way he'd been betrayed, Pete walked out of *The Zone* with new purpose. Mr. Kagor had called him his friend and given him the secret to *The Aggressor*!

Pete sprinted home, stopping only to catch his breath. He pushed the key in the lock and bolted up the stairs. If he'd paused for a moment and looked around, if he'd gone into the living room first, or his bedroom, then everything that happened later, might have been very different. But he didn't. Instead, he went straight to the bathroom.

Sliding back the mirrored doors of the medicine cabinet, he rummaged feverishly through the bottles and boxes for something. Eventually, his trembling fingers found what he was searching for. Opening a small plastic case, Pete held the black object up to the bathroom light. It was his father's old electric hair-trimmer.

"Your skull... as close to the sensors as possible... any gap can make all the difference." The words echoed in his head, over and over again, as he fumbled for the shaver socket underneath the draped bath towels.

14

Out of Control

Mrs. Clark had had the dullest day imaginable. Fighting tiredness, she'd been tapping in endless rows of names and addresses for a solid eight hours. Her eyes and fingers were sore and she had a blinding headache.

Walking wearily down Ferndown Road with a bag of shopping and Tommy in tow, she now had to deal with Peter. She wasn't looking forward to it. She hardly knew him these days. In a matter of weeks, he'd changed. Suddenly, he was acting like a delinquent.

She shut the front door, dumped her bag in the hall and went into the lounge. She screamed in horror and stood rigid in the centre of the room. Hearing her cries, Pete stepped out of the bathroom and came down the stairs.

"What's going on? What have you done?" she yelled.

"It's only a haircut," Pete began, putting his hands to his newly-shaven head.

"No," she cried. "In here."

It was only then that Pete saw what he should have noticed when he first came in. He looked around the living room aghast. It was as if a tornado had swept through the house. Books, coats, toys, contents of drawers and cupboards, were scattered everywhere.

Pete gasped. "It's not me, Mum. I haven't done anything. I've only been home a short while and I went straight upstairs and..."

"We've been burgled," cried Pete's mum. "And you didn't even notice!"

"I... I'm sorry," said Pete.

"And what have you done to your hair?" she said. "You look like a thug."

Tommy stared at his brother. "You look like a skull," he giggled.

"Least I'm not the village idiot," Pete snapped.

Tommy's face went red as he dissolved into tears.

"Peter. PETER!" His mum glared fiercely at him. "If your father was alive, he'd... he'd..."

"But he isn't, is he?" Pete snapped.

"Go to your room, NOW!" his mum yelled.

By the time the police had gone and Mrs. Clark had cleared up the mess, she had started to calm down a little. But Pete was feeling worse. He'd gone to his bedroom to find it ransacked too, but the only thing missing was the little notebook he'd found in the skip. Was that what the thieves had been after? Would someone really break in just to steal a notebook of computer game tips? Pete's thoughts were suddenly interrupted by Tommy creeping nervously into his room. He tugged the arm of Pete's shirt to get his attention.

"Peter, Peter, will you help me with my reading?"

"Shove off and play in the garden."

"But Peter..."

"I'm busy. Go and play in the garden." Pete raised his voice. "Go and find some glass to play with," he added cruelly.

Tommy ran out of Pete's bedroom.

Pete ran his hands across his shaven head and stared out of the window. The sun had almost set behind the small bank of tower blocks in the distance. Pete half turned his back to the glow and gazed across the long line of gardens. There was no one around, not even nosey old Mrs. Taylor, which made a change.

Pete's eyes rested for a moment on the sad patch of concrete where Dad's greenhouse had stood. He turned away. He was suddenly reminded of his dream, of the wrecked buildings and hunting through the rubble, searching for something, searching for what? Of course! The little red notebook... which was now missing. He shivered. His bad dreams were really getting to him. And for the first time, he began to wonder if they were linked to *The Zone*. Of course not. *The Zone* wasn't the problem. In fact, it was the best thing that had happened to him for a long time. The problem was everyone else.

CCRRAASSHH! Pete looked down at where Tommy was playing. A pane of glass had smashed on the ground at his feet. In a flash, it all came back. The accident. Smashing glass, his father flying through the windscreen, the sound of squealing brakes, screams, cries. Pete held his head in his hands, trying to rid himself of the noises and the images that followed.

"Tommy, TOMMY!" Pete roared as he bounded down the stairs and out of the back door.

"What the hell are you playing at?" He grabbed his brother and shook him fiercely.

Tommy's grin disappeared. "You told me to play with glass. It was only a joke, I was trying to make you laugh. You never laugh Peter, you never..." Tommy burst into tears.

"Laugh? I'll make you laugh, you idiot!" Pete ranted, shaking his brother so hard that Tommy began to scream.

"Stop it, Peter. STOP!" Hearing the commotion, Mrs. Clark had rushed out into the garden. She wrenched Pete away from his younger brother, leaving Tommy to race indoors, with tears streaming from his eyes.

"Peter... what is the matter with you?" she screamed at him.

But Pete didn't hear. He didn't want to hear. Without saying a word, he stormed up the stairs to his bedroom, pausing to knock his parents' wedding photograph off the shelf in the hall. Slamming the door shut behind him, he turned the key in the lock and stood with his back to the door. That would show her.

It wasn't fair. He was always getting the blame for everything. If only his father was alive, he wouldn't have let all this happen.

He stayed in his room for ages, just sitting on his bed, thinking, remembering. Eventually he heard his mother coming up the stairs.

"Peter... Peter," she called, turning the handle to the locked door. "Come on... let me in," she said. But Pete sat on his bed in silence. He didn't move. Let her worry.

It wasn't until he heard her heavy sigh and her footfalls on the stairs, that he got up. He had to get out. He needed to escape the claustrophobia of the house. Stopping to grab his flashlight, he pulled himself up onto the window ledge and pushed the window open.

Taking a deep breath, he swung down to the flat roof outside and scrambled over to the gutter. Then he took a deep breath before jumping to the ground. Not even pausing to look back and see if he'd been discovered, he ran... ran for what seemed like forever. By the time his aching lungs and legs begged him to stop, he found himself on the far side of the park. The sun had completely set now and the park was in darkness.

A thin veil of mist had started to rise from the

ground cloaking everything with a strange fuzzy whiteness. An owl hooted in the distance. The sound chilled Pete to the bone. He hadn't been out this late before, never alone. He didn't like it. He was scared. But he didn't want to go home.

Slumping onto the damp ground, he propped his lolling head up with his arms. For a long time, he tried to collect his scrambled thoughts but the sound of muffled voices in the distance brought him back with a start. The voices were all female and some way off, but they seemed to be getting closer. Pete looked all around. He didn't want anyone to see him, especially now.

Scrambling to his feet, he made his way along a dirt track for a few steps until he saw some shadows cast by a tiny copse of trees and bushes to his right. He pushed his way into the undergrowth and waited for the voices to disappear. They soon did.

He went to leave the thicket but found that he couldn't. He felt a prickly sensation on the back of his neck – as if he wasn't alone. Slowly, nervously, he flicked on his flashlight. He turned slowly, with the flashlight in his hand casting a thin beam of light on the bushes all around.

His gaze fell on an ancient, discarded bicycle wheel, rusted and bent with many spokes missing. He relaxed. Old bicycle parts don't have a presence now, do they? The flashlight swung past the wheel and down into a dip behind a small clump of bushes. Pete stopped in horror. In the shallow ditch he could just make out a limp, ghostly white hand.

15

Murder!

The pale face, drained of blood, and the arms and legs stuck out at unnatural angles, left no question that the person was dead. Pete dropped the flashlight and stared in horror. His stomach lurched. Suddenly he felt sick.

It was the body of a boy... Stefan Bremner.

Bending down to pick up his flashlight, Pete forgot everything else and raced as fast as he could back to Ferndown Road. He had to tell Mum. She'd know what to do. She'd make it all right.

When he reached the house, every window was dark. There wasn't a sign of life. Inside it was deadly quiet. She must have gone to bed early. He was just about to race up the stairs to her room, but something stopped him. With a stab of regret, he thought of how he'd refused to open his door.

She didn't even know he'd left the house. She'd be furious. And then there was the memory of the look on her face when he'd woken her before, her anger.

Pete sat down on his bed. He was home anyway. Inside his room, the terrors of the park seemed strangely distant. He was safe and that was all that mattered. For the first time in ages, Pete felt tired – totally and utterly exhausted. He pulled his shoes off, climbed under the duvet and laid his head on the pillow...

The next thing Pete knew, it was morning and the light was streaming in through the window. He looked at his bedside clock. 8:50. He'd missed assembly again for the second day running. Not that it mattered really, not compared with what he'd seen last night. But he wasn't going to think about that. Quickly he blotted it out. It hadn't really happened had it?

Rushing around the house, Pete gathered his school books. He left the house quickly and reached school just as assembly had finished and everyone was starting to file out for their classes. Pete joined them.

His class-mates were unusually quiet – even Graham Johnson. No one spoke to Pete, but he didn't care. What did they mean to him? A bunch of kids who probably couldn't even get past level one of *The Aggressor*.

Caught up in his own thoughts, Pete sat down, opened his exercise book and awaited Mr. Robertson's arrival.

Mr. Robertson entered the room with as serious an expression as Pete had ever seen on his wizened features. "Before I begin the lesson, I just want to say a few words. In the light of the terrible events of yesterday, I've got to tell you not to talk to any of the journalists hanging around outside the school. Please think of Fiona's family. If you do have any information about the murder, please speak to PC Tucker – he'll be in school all day."

Murder! The horror of the word brought back the terrible memories with a sudden rush... the pale face, the limp, twisted hand. Murder! Stefan Bremner was dead and he, Pete Clark, had stumbled across his body.

"Sir, can I be excused?" Pete begged.

Mr. Robertson nodded grimly and Pete ran out of the classroom and into the toilets. Slamming a cubical door shut, he retched and retched. He felt terrible.

Eventually he flung back the door, went over to one of the washbasins and splashed some water on his face. "Pull yourself together," he urged himself. "It's nothing to do with you. It wasn't your fault."

By the time Pete had calmed down enough to return to his classroom, he found it empty. Looking at his watch, he realized he'd missed the whole lesson.

He set off listlessly down the corridor towards an open door leading into the playground. Fresh air. He must have fresh air. Just as he went to walk outside, Mr. Robertson appeared from nowhere.

"Ah, Peter. There you are. Too overcome with the emotion of great literature to rejoin us were you?"

"No, I was..."

"Had a haircut I see," Mr. Robertson continued. "Won't need another one in a hurry, will you?"

For a brief moment, Pete was confused. He'd completely forgotten about his shaven head. "Yes sir, I er..."

"Come on," said Mr. Robertson. "I need a hand with some computer equipment."

Pete groaned silently, but he was grateful that Mr. Robertson hadn't quizzed him any further about his hair. Limply he followed the English teacher into the Computer Studies room and started shifting equipment according to Mr. Robertson's instructions. As he moved an ink jet printer, he spotted a magazine wedged underneath. The words on the open page caught his eye: *Can computers really read your mind?* He stopped dead.

"What's wrong?" Mr. Robertson asked, concerned.

"N... nothing Sir. I was just looking at that," Peter pointed. "Do you think computers can really read your mind?"

Mr. Robertson smiled. "It's an interesting article, a little technical for you perhaps, but food for thought. All about computers converting thoughts into digital signals."

Pete was puzzled, but intrigued. "Really?" he

said.

"Just imagine if all your thoughts and ideas could be downloaded onto a computer and stored on a hard disk. It could work the other way too – digital signals retrieved from the computer could be converted into thoughts and implanted in the brain. Just think what a breakthrough that would be," Mr. Robertson enthused, with a smile. "Doctors could treat shock and trauma victims, disabled people could have wheelchairs and even cars controlled by their mind instead of their hands and feet."

Pete shifted uncomfortably. "Really? Is that true? I mean, can computers *really* take thoughts out of your brain and use them?"

"Not now," Mr. Robertson smiled reassuringly. "The interface doesn't exist. I mean we haven't discovered a means of recording and interpreting the signals in the brain. We'd have to do that before we could download them onto a computer. But your brain and a computer aren't so very different. They both work on electrical impulses – although the brain is rather more sophisticated. But who knows what might be possible in the future..." Mr. Robertson paused. "It's certainly something to think about. A very interesting idea. Now let's get on and shift these computers."

"Okay," Pete replied and hesitated. He needed someone to confide in. Maybe Mr. Robertson was one of the few teachers who might just listen.

"Sir, just supposing, that a machine already

exists, one that reads your mind and plugs it into a computer... or even a video game. Would it be..."

"Come on now, Pete. Save your imagination for your next creative English class. Plug in that monitor and you can go."

Pete wavered. He desperately wanted to talk to someone who would understand all the terrible things that were happening to him. But it was obviously no good trying Mr. Robertson. He was just like every other teacher. Pete left the computer room confused and depressed. Who would believe him?

16

Questions, Questions

Pete didn't feel any better at lunchtime. He was sitting by himself in the dinner hall when a younger kid crept up to him.

"What do you want?" Pete asked, not meaning to sound rude, but creating the effect all the same.

"There's someone at the front gate... says he wants to see you," the kid stuttered.

"Okay, thanks," Pete muttered, leaving the table. It was Rick. "It's good to see you," Rick said.

Pete glanced up at Rick's face. It had always been pale, but now it was as if his skin was too tight for his bony features. His bloodshot eyes were staring out from oversized eye sockets. He looked awful.

"What do you want, Rick?" Pete asked warily, still upset about Rick's betrayal.

"I wanted to see how you were," Rick replied nervously.

"Yeah, sure," Pete glowered.

"What's wrong, Pete? I know we haven't seen much of each other recently, but we're still mates, aren't we?" he said. "What about all those games of *Jinza* and *Virtual Fighter*? They were fun, weren't they? Remember your first time on *The Aggressor*?" Rick was speaking rapidly, doing his best to be friendly, as if he was trying to make amends.

"I remember," scowled Pete. "I also remember that Mr. Kagor told me you're paid to be friends with people."

"Look, I know you're upset about the burglary..."

"What?" Pete looked shocked. "How do you know about that?"

"I... er... heard about it."

Pete was angry. Suddenly he knew. "It was you wasn't it? It was you who broke in!" he cried.

"What do you mean?" Rick tried to smile with these words, but Pete wasn't fooled.

"You burgled our house, just for a stupid notebook?" he shouted. "Why?"

Rick was silent, then he shrugged his shoulders. "Mr. Kagor made me do it, Pete. He wanted his notebook back. It had an important computer program written in it. You have to believe me."

"It was Stefan's," said Pete.

"No it wasn't," said Rick, suddenly confident. "Stefan stole it from Mr. Kagor."

"Why should I believe you? Why should I believe

a Virtual Addict?" Pete snarled. "That's what you are, aren't you? Have you been playing Virtual Murder as well?"

Rick's face went ghostly white.

"What do you mean?" said Rick. "Murder?"

"Don't you know?" said Pete. "Stefan's dead. He's been murdered." Rick hadn't known, Pete could see that. The fear in his eyes was unmistakeable.

"Oh no, not Stefan!" Rick trembled. "Pete, you don't know what's going on at *The Zone*. It's really heavy. In the room at the back of the Inner Zone, Mr. Kagor has this *Mindmaster* machine and—"

"Well, don't go back there," Pete butted in.

"Please Pete, listen. I have no choice, I'm trapped," Rick cried. His face was bleak, his eyes empty. "Look, if you help me, I mean, together we might be able to stop everything," Rick urged.

"No way," Pete shouted.

"But you must!"

"Whatever you do or say, I'm never going back to *The Zone* again, do you hear? NEVER!" Pete surprised himself with the force of his outburst.

Rick's hollow brown eyes flashed for a moment before he turned on his heels and quickly walked off without another word.

Pete sat through his afternoon lessons, barely listening to a word the teachers said. He thought about telling the police about Rick and the break-in, but knew he couldn't. He was scared. He was in too deep and after all, Rick had only stolen a notebook – a notebook that Pete himself had taken.

That evening, Pete watched the TV news. It mentioned Stefan's murder – how his body was found in the park and that the police were appealing for witnesses. Pete turned off the TV at that point. He couldn't go to the police, not now. What if they thought he had something to do with it?

But he couldn't stop thinking about Stefan. He hadn't liked him, and at times may have wished him hurt or out of the way, but never dead. Not in real life. His thoughts switched to the hours he'd spent zapping and blasting a computer-generated Stefan, and he flinched at the memory.

Pete dragged himself upstairs and started getting ready for bed. As he brushed his teeth he stared into the bathroom mirror.

The figure that stared back looked so different to the one he was used to. The lower half of his face was now dappled with pimples. A shadow of stubble was faintly visible on his shaven head.

"What's happened to me?" he heard himself say in a hushed whisper. "I look as bad as Rick." He suddenly thought of Mr. Kagor's words about Rick. "He can't leave the machines alone. He's a Virtual Addict."

Had he too become a Virtual Addict? For the first time since his dad had died, Pete wept. He wept until he'd run out of tears.

* * * * * * * * * * * * * * *

That night, Pete promised himself he would make a new start, just as he'd said to Rick. He'd stop going to *The Zone*, stop playing *The Aggressor*.

The following week was half term and Pete tried his hardest to go back to the way things were before *The Zone* had entered his life. But Tommy showed no signs of coming around. Ever since the incident with the broken glass, Tommy had ignored him. And nothing Pete did would make any difference. He did Tommy's chores, offered to play with him and help him with his reading, but each time, Tommy just walked off.

The closest Pete got to a conversation with his little brother was late on Tuesday morning.

"Your friend called round," Tommy said dully.

"Jez? When?"

"No, not Jez, the one with the earring. He left you this." Tommy thrust a folded piece of scrap paper into Pete's hand before scurrying off to his room. Pete unfolded the note.

Dear Pete,

We must talk. Things are pretty bad at The Zone. Mr. Kagor is very worried about you, especially after what happened to Stefan. He's very upset about Stefan and wonders if you know anything about who did it. Mr. Kagor is putting up a large reward for anyone with information about Stefan's death. Hope to see you soon. The games miss you!

Rick

Pete read and re-read the note. There was something wrong about it. Rick had seemed so scared when he last saw him, and now, in this letter, he sounded almost cheery. A warning sounded like a siren in the back of his head. However much Rick and Mr. Kagor were worried, if indeed they were, he couldn't, he *wouldn't* go back to *The Zone*.

The note must have bothered him more than he thought. That night, he lay in bed, wide awake. He couldn't sleep however hard he tried. He couldn't rid himself of the image of Stefan in the park.

2:25. Pete looked at the fluorescent numbers on his alarm clock. He shuffled downstairs for a glass of milk, recalling Rick's words and thinking things through. If the notebook was important enough for Mr. Kagor to force Rick into burgling Pete's house, what else might he do?

Pete stopped suddenly, milk bottle in hand. A terrible thought came into his head. What if Mr. Kagor had murdered Stefan? Pete's face felt hot and his heart was thumping. He wished he'd let Rick talk some more. He wanted to speak to him now. But that was impossible. He didn't know where he lived and he couldn't risk going to *The Zone*. He couldn't talk about any of this with Mum. He had never felt so alone in his life.

17

Something in the Attic

It was late by the time Pete got out of bed on Wednesday morning and the house was deserted. His mum was at work already and hazily, Pete remembered something about Tommy going to an adventure playground with a friend's family.

Pete felt awful. He was hungry, but he didn't want to eat anything. His head was fuzzy and he felt a dull ache behind his eyes. The prospect of another whole day on his own alone in the house loomed ahead of him. There was nothing to do. No one to talk to...

Then he saw his mother's purse lying there on the kitchen table. She must have forgotten to take it to work with her. He knew there wouldn't be much in it, but there'd be enough – enough for a couple of games at the arcade. But he'd promised himself he wouldn't go back. Even so, he couldn't stop thinking of *The Aggressor*. If only he could have one more go. It might make him feel better.

As he slurped down a bowl of cereal, he couldn't take his eyes off the purse. There it was tempting him. "Go on. Just once," it seemed to be saying. She'll never notice, Pete thought. I haven't been there for ages. Slowly his fingers moved across the wooden top to within inches of the purse. "Go on. You know you want to," a voice inside his head was urging.

Pete grabbed the purse with his right hand. No! With his left, he opened the top kitchen drawer. Throwing the purse inside, he slammed the drawer shut and breathed a sigh of relief. He'd won. He hadn't given in. But what now? He had to keep busy. That way he might be able to forget about *The Aggressor* for good.

Feeling suddenly more lively, he bounded upstairs and went into the bathroom. Avoiding the mirror, he picked up the old hair-trimmer from the shelf. "Only one place for this now," he said out loud. He'd made a decision. He would put it in the attic, with the rest of his dad's old things.

Pete pulled down the hatch to the attic and climbed up the metal ladder. Even as attics went, the place was a tip. Dusty suitcases, plastic bags with clothes spilling out, Tommy's old cot and stacks of cardboard boxes. Pete made a snap decision. He would clear up the attic – a job his mum had been thinking about doing for ages, but she'd never had the time or the energy.

Slowly, Pete started to sort through the old boxes. Brushing away the years of accumulated dirt and dust, he could see that most of the stuff had belonged to his dad. There was even a suitcase, labelled Master Roger Clark. His dad had hoarded things since childhood. Pete started to feel sad. Part of him wanted to get away from these sad reminders of his father. Part of him wanted to stay and see what he could find.

Pete had only managed to shift a couple of boxes when he heard footsteps coming up the stairs.

"Peter... Peter is that you?" It was his mum, home early. He'd hoped to have the whole attic clean as a surprise. Bother!

Mrs. Clark climbed up the rickety steel ladder and pulled herself up into the loft.

"What are you doing?" she said in a tired voice.

"I was just sorting out some of Dad's things for you," Pete started to explain, leaning back uncomfortably on an unfamiliar black guitar case, propped up against one of the rafters.

"That's your dad's," she said, pointing to where Pete was leaning. "You didn't know your father, used to play in a band, did you? Look." She flipped open the two catches to reveal a zebra-striped electric guitar.

Pete stared at the guitar for a moment. "Dad was a pop star?" he questioned.

"Not exactly," his mum said with a smile. "He

played the guitar a bit, that's all," she sighed. Pete knew she was thinking about his dad. "Your father hated throwing anything away. His whole history's up here." She paused. "Tommy won't be back for hours, so we might as well sort through some of this junk, eh?"

His mum's tone was more friendly than it had been for a long time. Pete smiled and nodded silently. Maybe things *would* get back to normal.

For the rest of the afternoon, they rummaged through the attic pulling out all sorts of things, long since forgotten. Most of it was new to Pete.

"Oh, you'll like this." Pete's mum started giggling as she pulled out a heavily beaten cardboard cover from a tatty brown case.

"I doubt you'll remember these. We used to call them records," she joked.

"I know what they are," Pete replied with a smile.

"Yes, but look inside."

Pete looked at the cover sleeve. Song titles leapt out at him in luminous green ink.

"*Filth 'n' Fury, Let's Riot, Kev's A Killer*. What's all this?" Pete asked.

"Turn it over," said his mum.

A band photo filled the whole of the other side of the sleeve. Five figures in skin-tight drainpipe trousers stared self-consciously from the picture. No, surely not. Pete shook his head and stared again at the photo before looking at his mum.

"Yes, third on the left," she grinned, shuffling closer to get a better look and gently placing her arm on Pete's shoulder.

Pete smirked. The smirk quickly grew into a snigger and the snigger into a full blown laugh as Pete stared at the picture of his dad, in a tight-fitting spangly top, dyed green hair and tartan trousers leering out of the photo at him.

"Eh? Whoever heard of the *Killer Ants* Mum? What were they like?" Pete managed to ask when his laughter subsided.

"Well, they weren't what you'd call 'easy listening'. They thought they were pretty mean," she replied. "They were pretty terrible actually, but there was something about your dad that I liked. I guess he didn't take himself as seriously as the rest."

"Dad wasn't serious about anything, was he?" Pete said.

"Oh, but he was. He was very serious about you boys. You meant everything to him. He would have hated seeing you and Tommy not getting on." Mrs. Clark stopped suddenly.

Pete stared at the floor.

"It's okay," she said, in a bright voice. "He'd be pleased to see us now." His mum smiled again. Pete looked over at the old record player he'd dusted earlier. Just as he was going to ask if they could resurrect it to play the record, the door bell rang.

"I'll get it," said Pete.

"No, I will." A hand clasped Pete's shoulder.

He turned and saw the warmth in his mum's eyes. "Things will be all right, Pete. We'll get through it, you know."

Pete choked back the tears that seemed to be coming from nowhere. "I'm sorry Mum... sorry about everything."

"Forget it. That's over." She paused for a moment as the bell rang again, more insistently this time.

"Okay, okay, keep your hair on," she shouted brightly as she ran down the stairs.

Pete grinned from ear to ear. That was one of Dad's phrases. Cheerfully, he continued tidying up the attic, leaving the *Killer Ants* album out, carefully propped up against the top rung of the ladder.

Pete's happy thoughts were suddenly interrupted by his mother shouting up the stairs.

"Peter! Come here quickly. Something awful's happened. It's Tommy..." she cried.

Pete felt his heart jump to his throat.

"What? What's happened?" he managed to force out in a shaky voice as he charged down the stairs.

His mother was standing at the foot of the stairs, fumbling in her handbag for a tissue. Behind her, framed in an open doorway, Pete could see two people. Police officers.

"Tommy's gone" said his mother, in a strange, strangled voice. "One minute he and Ben were playing in the sandpit... you know, the one in the adventure playground. The next minute he was gone." His mum began to sob. "Tommy's disappeared."

18

Tommy Come Back!

After that, Mum disappeared in a police car. Pete was left at home.

"Someone has to stay here," she said in a tearful voice. "Just in case..." Pete had nodded and agreed, but he had felt so useless. There was nothing he could do.

He couldn't face going back into the attic, so he wandered into the kitchen and tried washing up his dirty cereal bowl. Then he just wandered from room to room. He switched on the TV and flicked through the channels, but nothing grabbed his attention.

Time passed slowly and Pete began to fear the worst. Deep down he knew that Tommy couldn't simply have got lost or run away. He knew his brother too well. He may not be able to read, thought Pete, but he's not stupid.

Pete looked at his watch. Half past five. Mum had been gone three hours. He went back into the lounge, switched on the TV and sat, staring at the screen without taking anything in.

Then he must have dozed off because the next time he looked at his watch it was ten to eight. Pete wandered into the back garden. It was cold outside and the sun had almost disappeared. In the fading light, Pete began kicking Tommy's football back and forth against the fence.

"You watch my fence young man," Mrs. Taylor was standing by her back door.

Pete didn't reply.

"Everything all right?" Mrs. Taylor continued. "I saw your mother going in a police car. I hope there's no trouble..."

Pete eyed Mrs. Taylor coldly, wishing she would go away. "Tommy's missing," he said bluntly. He didn't need an interfering old busybody bothering him, especially now.

"Tommy?" cried Mrs. Taylor. She sounded genuinely surprised. "But I saw him in the High Street this afternoon with that hooligan friend of yours... the one with the earring."

Pete stared at her blankly, the words not registering at first. He looked up startled as the back door was shut firmly behind her.

"What was that, Mrs. Taylor?" he stammered, but Mrs. Taylor had gone back inside.

Tommy with that hooligan friend... the one with the earring. That's what she had said. RICK! Pete was rooted to the spot. Tommy had been with Rick. Terrible, awful images flooded his mind. He had to shut them out. He had to think straight. What did it mean? Where would Rick have taken him?

Pete could only think of one place – *The Zone*. His mind reeled. Tommy at *The Zone* with Mr. Kagor. It was all too horrible to imagine. He had to act quickly. Pete picked up the phone and rapidly tapped in the number of his once best friend. It was a gamble. What if Jez put the phone down on him?

A familiar voice replied. Pete's heart soared with relief.

"Hello Jez, it's Pete." Jez was silent. "Pete Clark."

"What do you want, Pete?" Jez's voice sounded cool from the other end of the phone.

"I know we've had some problems, Jez..."

"Some problems? You thumped me, you thug," Jez interrupted.

"Okay, I'm sorry about that, but something terrible's just happened and I need your help."

"Serves you right, hanging around that weird arcade."

"Jez, listen, please. This is *really* important. It's not about me. It's about Tommy."

Immediately, Jez's tone changed. "What's happened?" he asked.

"I think Rick from the arcade has taken him – kidnapped him."

"Kidnapped him? He can't have."

Pete started to get impatient. "Look, I haven't got time to explain things right now. Do you think you could stay up until I get back? If I don't call you back in a couple of hours, phone the police and tell them where I am."

"Okay, I'll do it, but where will you be?"

It was so obvious to Pete, he'd not thought to tell Jez.

"*The Zone*," he said. "I'm going back to *The Zone...*"

19

Dark is *The Zone*

Pete put his flashlight in his pocket and crept out of the house. Turning right, he walked briskly down the road, across the junction and up Hillside Avenue. It was almost dark by the time he reached the edge of the park, and he felt an uneasy, jittery sensation in the pit of his stomach. He couldn't face taking the short route across it at night, not since he'd found Stefan there.

He picked out a well-lit route across town until, at last, he came to the industrial estate. Not crossing the park meant his journey had taken almost an hour. He would have to get a move on.

He ran swiftly through the deserted ghost town of the industrial estate keeping as calm as he could. He sucked in his breath as the familiar black

98

warehouse cast a vast, eerie shadow in front of him.

The heavy entrance door was locked. No one seemed to be around. But Rick and Tommy just had to be inside. Where else could they be? He had to get in.

Pete crept around the building looking for a way in. There were no other doors. Suddenly he saw a metal fire escape leading right up to the roof. And just above, to the right, a skylight. Of course – that had to be the skylight in the ceiling of Mr. Kagor's workshop – *The Inner Zone*.

He climbed up the rusting stairs of the fire escape and inched himself along the roof until he reached the skylight window. He was in luck, it was open. Gently, he eased himself through the gap and stared down into the dark, empty room below. It was a long way down, but he jumped all the same, catching his hand on a nail as he fell. Ouch! A deep cut was etched into his palm.

Pete gritted his teeth and bandaged his hand with his handkerchief. Carefully, he picked his way across the workshop towards the door that led down into the arcade. As he passed the desk, he saw something that made the hairs on the back of his neck stand on end. A folder lay open, photos spilling out. On the top was a picture of his little brother, Tommy, playing with a friend in the playground.

"No... no!" Pete cried, picking it up to have a closer look. His mind was in turmoil. He couldn't think straight. But his thoughts were abruptly interrupted by a grinding, whirring noise from the computer terminal on the desk. Then he heard a louder, mechanical noise and he knew something was printing out. Without hesitating, Pete ripped the page from the paper stream. What he read caused his heart to start beating even faster.

```
Research Log: 20/5: 19.45

Rick failed to bring the boy here despite
his promises. Said he changed his mind and
let the kid go. This was his last chance.
Earlier threats were clearly ineffective.
Had no option but to deal with him in the
same way as Stefan. Interestingly, Rick was
a much harder mind to crack. Downloaded 75%
of his memory onto Mindmaster, but couldn't
access the rest. He refused to cross the
void which means retrieval is still
possible. Have stored what I can at Level 7.
Will try again tomorrow, if he survives. Not
sure he's worth it. His experiences appear
to be largely traumatic, so are probably
surplus to requirements.
```

Pete's mind swam. The meaning was hard to take in, but four words leapt out at him... *let the kid go*. Rick had let Tommy go! Pete's heart leapt with joy. Tommy was safe!

Pete stood up. He just wanted to get out of this place as quickly as possible. He couldn't climb back up to the skylight, the tiny barred window was far too small to squeeze through. He walked over to the door that led down into the arcade. Locked. Pete looked in despair at the hefty locks on the thick metal door. He'd never get out that way.

Pete looked around. Surely there was another way out. In a flash he remembered an open door with a bare room beyond. The door was shut now, but it wasn't locked. It was dark inside and Pete could hear a faint buzzing noise. He fumbled for a light switch on the wall. A single low-power bulb, high up in the ceiling, cast a pall of yellow light about the room. Pete shivered. The room was more full of shadows than anything else. Slowly, he stepped inside.

Like before, he saw a big white dust sheet draped over a mysterious bulk. Of course... Mr. Kagor's *Mindmaster* machine. And then he saw something else.

Lying completely motionless beneath the sheet was a figure. Its arms and legs were splayed out at uncomfortable angles. The colour drained from Pete's face and images of Stefan in the park flashed through his mind. His heart skipped several beats as he crept slowly towards the figure. It was wearing a headset wired up to the machine. No one would try to sleep like that. Through the gloom he realized it was someone he knew... someone that he knew very well... it was Rick.

20

No Turning Back

Pete bent over and felt for a pulse on Rick's wrist. He pressed his finger hard against one of the veins and waited.

"Come on Rick, you must be alive," he urged. There was a pulse but it was very faint. He looked hard at Rick's face. Too many hours in the arcade had always given it a sickly pallor. But this time it was white... lifeless.

What had been done to him? Gently, Pete tried to unfasten the clasp on the headset. But it was stuck tight, locked to his head. This was Mr. Kagor's doing. Pete knew that without a doubt. He also knew this was what had happened to Stefan before Pete had found him dead, dumped in the park. It was too late for Stefan, but what about Rick?

Suddenly the words of the computer printout came back to him – Mr. Kagor's research log. Had Rick's memories really been downloaded onto a games machine, onto the *Mindmaster*?

Pete tried telling himself this was nonsense. Impossible. But as he stared at Rick's limp, lifeless face, he knew it had to be true. The words of the log came back to him... *Downloaded 75%... couldn't access the rest... retrieval is still possible.* Rick stood a chance! But how? Through the machine. Through the *Mindmaster*.

Pete took hold of the dustsheet. The material was heavy and felt rough to his fingers. The cut in his hand was really starting to ache. He counted.

One.

This is dangerous.

Two.

Tommy's safe. That's all that matters.

Three.

Turn back. Leave now...

Four.

Rick is dying.

Five!

Off came the dustsheet.

Mindmaster looked disappointingly amateur – worse than *The Aggressor*. There wasn't much to it. A large black box which looked more like an ancient amplifier than a sophisticated games console. It was perched on top of a couple of plastic crates with wires trailing from the back in a tangled mass. On the floor, on a grey rubber mat, there was a headset, identical to the one on Rick's head and a freeglide, wireless joystick.

Pete walked onto the mat and picked up the headset. It was similar to the one that came with *The Aggressor*, only heavier. He slipped it over his head, fastened the clasp and looked down at the console. There was no coin slot and just one lever with a series of numbers beside it etched into the metal. This was like a lot of machines in the arcade. The lever selected the levels of play, from 1 to 13.

Pete pulled the lever down to number 1 and went to pick up the joystick, but it wouldn't budge. Pete bent right down and tried again. It still wouldn't shift. Ignoring the pain from the cut, he pulled again, this time with both hands. Nothing. He cursed – the game was useless without a joystick. Then he tried to take off the helmet, but it wouldn't move. The clasp at the back was locked tight.

As he tried to wrench it off a second time, his eyes were suddenly dazzled by bright, flashing lights and a set of 3D graphics projected themselves first in front of him, then all around. The headset had come to life. Solid letters hung in mid-air around him. Instinctively he stepped back to get a better view.

MINDMASTER

© M. Kagor

COLLECT THE GOLD KEYS
YOU HAVE THREE LIVES

A series of blue numbers hanging in the air to the left of him showed the game levels, with a flashing cursor at the bottom next to number 1. He reached down again for the joystick, but still it wouldn't come free.

He looked up again to see the cursor slowly travelling upwards 1... 2... 3... Pete stared, suddenly scared. He had no control over this game. *"Get out of here!"* his brain screamed at him, and he started to wrestle with the headset again. But the clasp still wouldn't budge. He tried to step off the grey mat beneath his feet, but some invisible force yanked him back. And all the time the cursor was climbing upwards 4... 5... 6... until it stopped at number 7.

Level 7. This was the place where Rick's memories were stored. But what was he supposed to do now? He couldn't play the game – the joystick was bust. He couldn't stop the machine – the helmet was locked. He was trapped – trapped inside the *Mindmaster*.

21

Mindmaster

Then the game began. At first, Pete's fears seemed unfounded. *Mindmaster* threw him onto familiar territory – streets, houses, gardens, shops. It moved fast, but it wasn't scary. The machine seemed to respond to his movements and speech. Leaning towards the console and walking on the spot moved him forward.

He was looking for golden keys. He knew this from the solid letters that had hung in mid-air. The keys weren't hard to find and all he had to do was reach out and take them.

Every time he picked one up, a series of images filled the screen and a variety of wonderful sensations filled his mind and flowed through his body. It was wonderful – like a magical mixture of happiness, excitement, peace and confidence all rolled into one. If only he felt like this in real life, he thought. Nothing would ever bother him again.

Suddenly Pete spotted a key in the road. Darting out to grab it, he heard a car's brakes squeal. He saw an image of someone who looked like a younger version of Rick in the front seat. He was suddenly thrown sideways, as if the car had caught him a glancing blow.

A flash of pain seared through his right arm. Impossible, thought Pete. He wasn't even wearing a VR glove. A dull ache was spreading from his arm all over the right side of his body and with it his mood began to change. The magical feeling was draining away leaving a terrible sense of emptiness and despair in its place. Then came the fear. This was getting frightening.

He pulled at the headset again. He had to get it off, even if it meant tearing at the straps, ripping them out, cutting his flesh. But the machine was in control and it wasn't letting him go. The scene in front of him changed abruptly. He was inside a room. It wasn't large but everything in it looked slightly larger than normal, like an ordinary room must seem to a small child.

A man was standing opposite him, much taller than Pete, with a brutal expression on his hard face. Pete turned to run. He had to escape. But he was in a corner. He was trapped.

"It's only a game, it's only a game," he tried telling himself.

"It's nothing more than you deserve, Rick," the man was saying.

"Rick?" Pete yelled. "I'm not Rick." The man raised his arm and brought it down hard. THWACK! A clenched fist caught Pete full on the jaw. He ducked to avoid a second blow. Too slow. CRUNCH! Another very real punch jolted him. Pete stumbled onto the mat, his brain scrambled. More blows rained down on him before the sound of a woman screaming stopped the assault.

As Pete lay groaning on the floor, waiting for the next blow, the truth suddenly dawned. These were Rick's memories, downloaded onto the machine and now being replayed as a grotesque arcade game.

"Give up!" the man snarled. An icon appeared in mid-air with the words *PRESS TO GIVE UP* flashing underneath. With a huge sense of relief, Pete lifted his arm, but he stopped short. Rick's memories were still trapped inside the machine. He couldn't give up now.

Instantly, he was back at the beginning and the punches began again. They hurt twice as much this time.

After the beating was replayed a third time, Pete collapsed. The pain was unbearable now. He lay motionless, unable to touch the icon that hung in mid-air just beyond his reach. How long he lay there was impossible to tell, but he gradually became aware of a new message. The light hurt his swollen eyes, but he could read the words.

MEMORIES ACCESSED
DOWNLOAD OR RETRIEVE?

Groggily he searched for the right word in his brain... retrieve... retrieve... retrieve... forcing it to the forefront of his mind. A grinding noise echoed inside his head. Suddenly his view went blank, then his eyes were filled by a dizzy sequence of images, like a video recorder rewinding at high speed. He shut his eyes and clamped his hands over his ears. The noise was deafening.

Silence came suddenly and Pete staggered shakily to his feet. The headset seemed to have switched itself off. There were no more images in front of his eyes and he could see the room clearly through the headset. He turned to see Rick starting to move.

"Rick, it's me, Pete. Rick!" Pete shouted as loudly as he could.

Rick stood up and Pete saw the fear in his eyes. Still unable to move from the grey rubber mat, Pete watched as Rick pulled off his headset and threw it to the floor. Then he scurried out of the room like a frightened animal. Pete fought the rising nausea in the pit of his stomach.

Surely, Rick couldn't... wouldn't leave him, not after he'd saved him? Then Pete heard the sound of bolts and chains rattling downstairs. A door slammed. Rick had gone.

And as the awful truth sank in, Pete looked in horror at the lever on the *Mindmaster* console. It had moved all the way up to the top. Level 13.

22

Into the Void

The game began again but it was faster this time. He was moving along unknown streets, passing unfamiliar faces, still looking for keys. But this time he couldn't find any.

Suddenly he saw something he recognized – a house just like the one his grandad had lived in. Like a lightning flash, it triggered a distant memory – himself as a child in his grandad's garden. Then he saw a swing – his old swing in his own back garden. His mum was there too with a baby in her arms. Tommy. His first memory of his little brother. *Mindmaster* was coaxing his memories from him, memories he hadn't even realized were there.

The pace was increasing – more familiar people, more familiar places, each one triggering a high speed memory. Faster and faster still, memories flooded his mind, as his whole life was played out at breakneck speed in a random sequence right before his eyes.

He couldn't think straight. He tried, but he didn't have enough brain power left to concentrate on thinking. His mind was filled with images – images of himself, of his family and friends, of places and things. He had no control. They were escaping and he couldn't call them back. He focused momentarily on the image of a notebook. *The notebook*. The one he'd found in the skip.

Then it was gone and the dizzying images returned, with even greater intensity. And the noise in his ears was rising. It wasn't just the volume that was deafening, it was the complexity of the sounds, as if hundreds, thousands, of soundtracks were being played all at once.

And then, out of the chaos, one single figure began to grow slowly larger and brighter. The giddy swirl of jumbled images began to fade and disappear leaving a dark, empty void. Pete's mind began to clear and the figure became a man with dark brown hair, standing on the far side of the void. He could concentrate at last. He stared at the figure. "Dad!" Pete cried. "Is it really you?"

"Come on Pete!" His father held his arms out wide. Pete stretched as far as he could. He wanted to touch his dad's hands, wanted to feel their warm, safe presence. The *Mindmaster* had terrified him. He wanted comfort now. And there was Dad, good

111

old Dad, to look after him.

Pete stepped forward. He could feel the tears in his eyes. Thank goodness Dad was here to rescue him from this madness. Just as Pete went to take the final step into the blackness, something stopped him. One line from the notebook – *never cross the void*. The words seemed to scream inside his head. *Never cross the void.* He stopped, his foot hovering in mid-air above the darkness.

"Come on Pete," his father called, still smiling. "We'll be late for your match if we don't go soon."

Pete hesitated. *Never cross the void.*

Late for the match? But he'd been dropped from the team. The last time Dad had said those words was the day of the accident – the day his dad had died.

His father's face started to grow stern. "Come on now, Peter. There's not much time left. We'll be late."

"No, I won't!" Pete screamed. "I've been dropped from the team... and you..." He paused. His mouth felt dry. "You're not my dad. My dad's dead! You're just a copy of him... an imposter..."

With tears streaming out from underneath the headset, Pete gazed at the computer-generated copy of his dad.

The scene changed. He was now standing by the main road between Elmwood and Telfer's Heath – the very place where... Pete watched in horror as a red estate car sped along the tarmac. Suddenly, he was inside the car. He turned his head. His dad was

112

sitting beside him. "Okay, okay. I'll get you there on time. Don't worry." His dad smiled at him.

The accident was replayed in slow motion. The screams, the smashing glass, the impact, just as it had happened in real life. Tears of pain rolled down Pete's face and a small, familiar icon flashed insistently PRESS TO GIVE UP.

The accident began again. The pain was more excruciating this time and the icon grew in size. Pete's hand began to move from his side. He couldn't stand any more and just before the moment of impact, he lunged at the icon hanging in mid-air. He had to stop this, whatever the cost.

The blood-soaked handkerchief bandage caught on the sharp edge of the console just before his hand reached the icon. As it cut into the raw wound, he lurched backwards, howling in agony. He felt dizzy, as though he was about to pass out. But he was no longer inside the car. The icon had gone and all Pete could see was his father standing beside the dark void. This time he was waving goodbye.

"Dad!" Pete shouted as everything slowly turned black.

Drained of all energy and emotion, Pete fell to the ground. A sharp click at the back of his neck brought him to his senses. The catch on the back of the headset snapped open. He was free.

Pete began to stumble to his feet, but his legs were too weak and he fell crashing to the floor. One single thought blazed through his brain. He had to destroy the *Mindmaster*. Dragging himself to his feet and with every last ounce of strength in his body, he lifted the console up, almost above his head. His arms were shaking, but he held it there, and with a last surge of strength he let it go.

The console smashed to the ground and shattered into pieces. Pete watched without emotion. Then he fell to the ground and without feeling anything, hit the back of his head hard on a sharp edge of the black, metal casing.

There was a faint crackle, a few tiny sparks and a thin wisp of blue smoke. It was the end of *Mindmaster*. Pete smiled and let himself slip into unconsciousness.

23

Safe at Last

When Pete's eyes opened, he was in hospital. His vision was blurred, but he could just make out two people standing over him.

"Hello Peter," his mother said gently. "How are you feeling?" Pete tried to sit up, but a dull thud at the back of his head stopped him from moving.

"I'm okay, but what about Tommy?" he croaked.

"Tommy's fine," she answered. "He made his way home all by himself. Mrs. Taylor found him sitting on the doorstep. It was Jez who told us where you'd gone. He phoned the police. Oh Pete, you had us all so worried."

Keeping his head on the pillow, Pete looked around as best as he could. A large trolley of electronic equipment stood beside his bed. "What's all that?" he asked in alarm.

"Careful, Peter. It's best if you don't move too much," came a voice. Squinting, Pete could just make out the face of a doctor. "It's okay," the doctor went on. "We've just been monitoring your condition while you were unconscious."

Pete drifted off to sleep. Then, later in the afternoon, he awoke to a new face in front of him. It was Jez.

"Your mum's gone to collect Tommy. She said it was all right to come in for a minute," Jez said uncertainly. "You know you've uncovered something huge. The whole industrial estate has been cordoned off."

"Thanks for calling the police," Pete said.

"I waited two hours like you said," Jez said. "I was so worried I just played *Jinza* to keep me... er, sorry Pete." Jez's voice faltered. "I guess you don't want to hear about arcade games."

"That's okay, Jez. I'm the one who should be saying sorry."

"Let's forget it, eh?"

Jez said goodbye, and the next thing Pete knew, Tommy came bouncing into the room.

"Peter! Peter! Is your hand okay? Ben at school says they might have to cut it off with a saw."

"No, my hand's fine," Pete assured him.

"So you can play in goal while I shoot? Great!" Tommy punched the air with joy.

Pete was allowed home a week later. On his last day in hospital, he spent several hours explaining everything to two police officers. They were kind and patient, letting him tell his story before asking any questions.

"You have nothing to worry about now," the police woman said at the end. "Mr. Kagor's been arrested and he'll be standing trial for Stefan's murder."

"But what about *Mindmaster* and what happened to Rick... what nearly happened to me?"

The police woman smiled patiently. "Just concentrate on getting better, Peter."

"But..."

"You know, you should have come to us as soon as you had concerns," she said.

"But I was scared," Pete said. "I didn't think anyone would believe me."

"You mustn't think that," she said in a quiet, kindly voice. "If you're telling the truth, we'll believe you." She nodded understandingly. "Well, you can put all that behind you now, can't you?"

But I've told you the truth about *Mindmaster*, he thought, and you don't believe me. You don't believe a word of it. But he didn't say anything. Instead he nodded and smiled weakly.

* * * * * * * * * * * * * * *

Next term Pete started soccer training as soon as he could, determined to regain his place on the school team. One night, on his way home from football practice, he caught sight of the headline of the local newspaper: *Arcade Owner Jailed for Life*.

When he got home, he found his mum's copy of the paper and feverishly scanned the article.

Arcade Owner Jailed for Life

Martin Kagor, 43, was sentenced yesterday to life imprisonment for the murder of local teenager Stefan Bremner, 16.

Mr. Kagor, proprietor of video games arcade *The Zone,* had employed Bremner as a security assistant. The circumstances of death were unusual, but a post mortem showed that the teenager died of severe head injuries. Mr Kagor remained silent throughout the trial, but forensic evidence was sufficient to prove Mr Kagor guilty of murder. There was no one else involved.

Bremner's mother said she was pleased that justice had been done. "Stefan was a fine lad with a bright future in front of him. He was a model son, a lovely boy who never hurt a fly."

The Zone, which has now closed, was a popular haunt for local youngsters, providing a wide variety of the latest video arcade games. There were also a number of unlicensed machines that Kagor himself had built.

Very little is known of Martin Kagor. He was a newcomer to the area, a quiet man who, according to neighbours, kept himself to himself.

However, now that the trial is over, some bizarre new facts are emerging, giving the case an almost sinister twist. A former colleague, who wishes to remain anonymous, claims that Martin Kagor had made huge advances in developing a communication link between the human brain and the computer. He also suggests that Kagor's own unpatented video games were working models of his work in this field.

Could this be true? There is evidence that Kagor received regular consignments of powerful electronic components possibly including stolen computer chips. Local teenager and regular games player Steve Rodway certainly thinks there is something in the story. "Those games were weird. They could read your mind, like the machine was stealing your thoughts and playing with them."

But experts in the computer world are less than convinced. "This is fantasy stuff," said Dr. Geoffrey Blundell, author of a recent article *"Can Computers Read Your Mind?"* "What is possible in theory has not been achieved in fact. Not yet."

Pete didn't read any more, he didn't need to. He knew what had happened. He knew the truth, but there was no point wasting valuable time telling anyone. It was all in the past. *Mindmaster* was destroyed and Mr. Kagor was in prison.

* * * * * * * * * * * * * * *

It was some months on before Pete was to get a last reminder of *The Zone*.

"Here," said Tommy, handing Pete a letter from the pile that had dropped through the letter box.

The handwriting was unfamiliar. Pete puzzled over who it could be from as he ripped open the envelope.

Dear Pete,

Guess you'll be surprised to hear from me after all this time! I'm living in Scotland with my aunt now – as far away from The Zone as possible.

I'm sorry I ran out on you like that. I didn't mean to leave you but I had to get out. I was scared. But I phoned the police. Did you know that?

I owe you one. I'll never forget it. Keep up your football, and stay away from arcades. See you sometime.

Rick

So Rick hadn't completely deserted him at *The Zone* that night. He had always wondered what had happened to him and now that he knew, Pete felt relieved. He'd been disappointed by Rick, but he'd never wanted to think badly of him. As Pete thought back to the terrible images of Rick's life, he felt sorry for him. But Pete didn't dwell on Rick for long, as his thoughts were disturbed by a tug on his sleeve. It was Tommy.

"Cat... and... mouse... want... a... pet," said Tommy, pointing to each word in his reading book.

Pete yawned and smiled. Tommy's reading was still painfully slow, but he was miles better. "That's great," said Pete. "How about a game of football?"